THE FIRST POWER

CHRISTIAN FRANCIS

BASED ON THE SCREENPLAY BY
ROBERT RESNIKOFF

978-1-916582-95-8 (eBook)
978-1-916582-66-8 (Trade Paperback)
978-1-916582-67-5 (Jacketed Hardcover)

 ECHO ON PUBLISHING

Contents

Foreword
Lou Diamond Phillips

1989.

The year this book is set but also the year we filmed the movie that is the inspiration for the novelization. The film would not premiere until April 6th of 1990. Adding to the zeitgeist of the moment, Richard Ramirez, The Night Stalker, was convicted and sentenced to death in 1989. Not as random a connection as you might think but more on that later.

As is mentioned in the book, Detective Russell Logan is of mixed heritage (though I'm not sure he was originally created that way) which would be unexceptional in a multicultural city like Los Angeles. His ethnic ambiguity would allow him to walk any street, blending into any neighborhood, a perfect and prototypical denizen of The City of Angels.

For me, as a mixed-race actor and fairly new to LA, my casting in the film was certainly a milestone, a plateau achieved, if you will. It was one of the first times in my career where the ethnicity of the character had no bearing on me playing the part. Not only that, it was a feature film and the leading role! I was especially pleased that the powers-that-be saw no reason to change his last name (Logan, very Scots/Irish) to justify me playing the role. After all, my legitimate last name is Phillips and I was born Lou Diamond Upchurch, even more Anglican. I made this joke in the movie Easter Sunday with Jo Koy – "I'm part Scots/Irish but did Mel Gibson put me in Braveheart? Nooooo!"

At any rate, I was proud to achieve 'cross-over artist' status, a new term for actors who could cross ethnic boundaries, I'm sure coined by the media and an industry that likes their boxes neat and tidy. My eternal thanks to Robert Resnikoff for his open-mindedness and vision. I also believe my casting was in large part due to our producer, Dave Madden, who I had recently worked with on Renegades with Kiefer Sutherland. It is still my belief that a culture change in our industry is championed by those decision makers behind the camera as much as it is by the aspirational and inspirational faces that we see on the screen.

I must say, at this point, when contemplating the character of Russell Logan, I find it highly interesting that novelist Christian Francis chose to age him up for the book. It is a totally legitimate choice and I'm intrigued by what that accumulated cynicism and world weariness would bring to the character, especially considering the horrors he would have experienced over a longer career. I've actually mentioned to Dave Madden how interesting it would be to play the character now at my age. This choice alone justifies a reason to novelize the film (along with a fresh perspective and the details that only the written word can convey) but also speaks to the potential of a sequel, which I have long thought the movie deserves. To Bob, Dave and any other potential exec...I'm available.

Given that we're still talking about this film, the legion of fans who discovered it after its initial release, and that the IP is still as viable as it is, I am more convinced than ever that the movie was ahead of its time. Bob Resnikoff was able to blend a number of genres into a completely unique and original film that borrowed but built upon the appeal of its predecessors. Those hyphenated films (dramedies, horror-comedies, rom-com thrillers) would find greater success in the 90s and beyond as audience tastes expanded and diversified. So how did we get to the nexus in 1989 where Resnikoff was able to envision a horror-occult-serial-killer-action thriller? The mile markers are actually not that difficult to map, Bob just knew where he was going.

The phenomenon of the serial killer grew rapidly across the nation through the seventies and eighties but it flourished especially in California. I'm assuming it's much more comfortable to murder on warm nights.

And in the land of Hollywood, a number of killers gained celebrity status. Randy Kraft, The Scorecard Killer, had a spree from 1972 to '83. 1979 saw both William G. Bonin, The Freeway Killer, and partners Lawrence Bittaker and Ray Norris, known collectively as The Toolbox Killers, gain notoriety. There were many more.

But even in a crowded field, there were those who achieved near legendary and mythic status, whose exploits were so horrific that they created widespread fear and paranoia and infected the national psyche for years following their capture. The following two cases had a direct connection and influence on the film The First Power.

Like Bittaker and Norris, The Hillside Strangler (later pluralized) was actually a team and their reign of terror lasted from 1977 to '78. The uncle and adopted nephew pair, Angelo Buono Jr. and Kenneth Bianchi were responsible for the deaths of ten young women in Los Angeles with two more being killed by Bianchi alone. During my research and preparation to play Detective Logan, I had the incredibly good fortune to spend some time with the lead investigator on the case, Detective Bob Grogan.

Grogan was a gruff and gregarious character who could've stepped right out of a 70s cop flick like The French Connection. I liked him instantly. Constantly monitoring a police scanner in his car, he took me on a 'ride-along' in LA in hopes of visiting an active crime scene. After several hours of simply cruising, (with the occasional pause to chat with hookers) Bob turned to me apologetically and said, "I'm sorry, Lou, no one's getting killed in LA tonight."

I assured him that I was grateful no one was meeting a violent end. He took me to the morgue instead. Having never been in one, it was shocking and sobering to say the least. It gave me much needed real-world context when films and film characters can often be cavalier about death. Many years and many cop performances later, I have always tried to imbue the characters with the proper respect and gravitas the job deserves, based largely on the memory and impact of that night. Thanks, Bob.

And then there was Richard Ramirez, The Night Stalker.

Between 1984 and 1985, Ramirez murdered at least 14, some of whom he raped and tortured. He was finally apprehended on August 31, 1985, not by the police but by an angry mob who recognized him from his wanted poster. At his sentencing in 1989, the presiding judge said that Ramirez exhibited "cruelty, callousness and viciousness beyond any human under-standing." He was sentenced to death but while awaiting execution, he died instead of complications from B-cell lymphoma on June 7, 2013.

Seemingly in keeping with the judge's observation, The Night Stalker case introduced yet another twist to the serial killer lexicon – the occult. Ramirez often left pentagrams at the crime scenes and proudly confessed to a fascination with satanic worship. No wonder that Ramirez was the primary inspiration for Patrick Channing, The Pentagram Killer, in The First Power movie and now novelization.

Incidentally, it's worth mentioning that Ramirez gained near rock-star status with groupies crowding the court room during his trial just to get a glimpse of him. While incarcerated, he received thousands of fan letters from women who professed love and lust for him despite his heinous crimes. Accordingly, Bob Resnikoff, Dave Madden and I met with a real rock star during the casting phase of the film: Michael Hutchence, the dynamic and ultimately tragic lead singer of INXS, came in to potentially play Channing. While Michael certainly had the requisite charisma and presence, Bob finally decided that the role of Channing required the nuance and complexity of a seasoned actor. The wonderful Jeff Kober was absolutely the best choice.

In yet another odd off shoot to The First Power legacy, I would go on to portray Richard Ramirez in a 2016 film written and directed by the brilliantly talented Megan Griffiths. While Ramirez is a real-life villain, the film, aptly titled The Nightstalker, is a fictional story that finds lawyer Bellamy Young trying to get Ramirez to confess to another crime that a client of hers is falsely accused of. The conceit itself is not only intriguing, but also firmly rooted in real assumptions since Richard never confessed to all his crimes. Hence the 'at least' in his body count. I portray Richard at the end of his life, wasting away from the lymphoma that would ultimately claim him. It was one of the deeper dives in my history of researching roles, rivaling the work I did on another Richard – Ritchie Valens in La Bamba.

Again, as with Bob Grogan, I was privileged to work with someone who was there and who could give me the real scoop. Lieutenant Gil Carillo was one of the co-leads of the task force that was formed to track down The Nightstalker and his work led to identifying Ramirez, ultimately leading to his capture. Gil would go on to personally interview Ramirez five times and he graciously shared his insight with me. On the first day of filming, we invited Lt. Carillo to the set. I could not have been prouder and more gratified when he told me I 'nailed it.'

Some of you may be aware that, not long after in 2019, Bellamy and I would go on to work together in the television series Prodigal Son where Michael Sheen plays – wait for it – a serial killer! And totally by coincidence, my character was Detective Gil Arroyo, a not-so-distant echo of Detective Gil Carillo. Six Degrees of Desanguination!

But back to Richard Ramirez and 1989. Richard's explicit inclusion of the occult in his crimes only exacerbated the terror people already felt when faced with the horrific reality of serial killers in our midst.

Demonic influence would certainly explain how a mere human being could become so evil. Tangentially, I think this fear can be linked to the phenomenon of Satanic Panic in the 80s and 90s where there were over 12,000 cases of unsubstantiated abuse arising from demonism or the occult, most famously in the McMartin preschool trial. (Interestingly enough, there is a resurgence of these ritualistic conspiracy theories courtesy of the internet.) Again, perhaps the collective consciousness that gave rise to these suspicions can be traced back to the cinema with films like The Exorcist in 1973 and The Omen in 1976 lending credence to the Devil dabbling in our everyday lives.

And so, to my mind (never having actually talked to him about it,) I believe Robert Resnikoff took all of these disparate ingredients, both real and surreal, tossed them into a blender and came up with the fabulous concoction that is The First Power. (I would also include in this Venn Diagram of Death, James Cameron's seminal 1984 film The Terminator, since it introduced the most amoral and inexorable killer since Bruce the Shark in Jaws.)

What I find fascinating is that our preoccupation with the Dark Side has not abated but, rather, seems more popular than ever. Horror films and television shows have seen a resurgence. Police procedurals are perennial. Documentaries on serial killers continue to unearth grisly details. And True Crime podcasts have garnered larger and larger audiences. Certainly, there is entertainment value, depending on your definition, but it goes beyond morbid fascination, vicarious thrills and jump scares.

There are fundamental questions that I think, even subconsciously, we want answered. Crimes of passion aside, what makes the criminal mind tick? And, in the case of serial killers, absent the influence of Satan himself, what makes a seemingly normal human being abandon all morality, compassion and empathy, even the simplest sense of right and wrong?

By studying these cases, contemplating them, maybe even understanding them, do we think we can prevent such heinous and horrific crimes against humanity? At the very least, can increased knowledge and awareness insulate and protect us from Evil? Turning the mirror on ourselves, what would it take for your own mind to snap and descend into madness?

Questions without definitive answers, to be sure. And maybe there are some things we really don't want to know.

Perhaps Stephen King, the Master of the Macabre, sums it up best –

"Monsters are real, and ghosts are real, too. They live inside us and sometimes, they win."

Happy reading.

Lou Diamond Phillips

Introduction
Robert Resnikoff

It was in the early 70s when I first began playing with the idea that would eventually become my 1990 film *The First Power*. Just out of film school at the University of Southern California, I was living the life of the screenwriter portrayed by William Holden in Billy Wilder's *Sunset Boulevard* – flat-broke, tiny Hollywood apartment, desperately groping for a script idea that could help me make it big. One of my stories seemed to have possibilities - a variation on the Greek myth of Orpheus descending into the underworld to retrieve his dead love, Eurydice. My Orpheus was a grizzled New York Jewish homicide detective who had to go into the lower depths to capture a serial killer. The story was called *Sheol*—the Hebrew name for hell. After a couple of nightmare-plagued evenings, I decided it would probably work better as a novel and wrote it down in my little notebook of ideas to be returned to later.

L.A. at that time was hopping. A new wave of American films. An exploding music scene. Despite Manson, hippiedom was still going strong. For a New York kid raised on pastrami sandwiches and pizza, the health food stores were a revelation. I especially liked the oatmeal raisin cookies and wholewheat brownies– the least healthy items on the shelves. My favorite of these haunts was a store called *Erewhon,* a mecca for young actresses whose stock in trade meant keeping their bodies in perfect shape. The walls of the place were a helter-skelter of ads and announcements, and one day a blue mimeographed page caught my eye – it read: *"Are you interested in radionics?"* Since searching for movie ideas meant casting a wide net, I had come across radionics in an old book that said it was an arcane form of medical quackery based on a little black box invented by Dr. Albert Abrams. The way it worked was that you put a patient's lock of hair or a drop of blood into the box and it would supposedly give electrical readings that showed the health of the body's organs. I loved that idea–I thought it could be a great Film Noir!

I sent off my check for $25—a fortune in those days, but hell, it was a business expense—and a week later, received a cryptic note with the address of a downtown hotel and a Saturday morning meeting time in two weeks. There was no other information, and as this was decades before the internet, there was no way to find out any more about what I might be getting myself into. But hey, I had done weirder things in my life, and as the days passed, I had almost forgotten about the whole thing.

Then the night before the meeting I had a strange dream. In the dream, I and a group of people were seated on the floor of a large room. A man stood at a podium—he had thinning brown hair and wore a black turtleneck sweater. He pointed his finger at me and I was suddenly *lifted high into the air* and sent floating around the room as I shouted - "<u>*This is real, it's all real!*</u>" I woke up panting. Trying to catch my breath, I laughed—dreams, go figure.

The next morning, I drove to the address I'd been sent. It was a typical downtown hotel for business travelers, nothing out of the ordinary. Inside the hotel, I was led into a conference room where a group of fifty people was already seated. After a short while, a man entered, obviously the group's leader. He had *thinning brown hair and was wearing a black turtleneck*—it was the guy from my dream! Again, this was years in advance of the internet and there was absolutely no chance that I had ever heard or seen this individual before.

I was stunned. The world I lived in had no room for a phenomenon like dreaming about something and then having it happen exactly like it did in the dream! I was a committed skeptic, a total atheist who at 16 had gone off to an Ivy League college and majored in mathematics. Raised in a left-wing family, I had been taught to believe religion was the opiate of the masses. And despite nearly giving my parents a heart attack by going off to film school, I still considered myself rigorously logical and rational. But at that moment, sitting in that conference room, the only hypothesis I could come up with was that some part of my consciousness was independent of time and space. But how was that possible?!

To test my hypothesis, I began gobbling down 'spiritual literature' to see if anyone else had ever had an experience like mine. I also started engaging with this group and its leader. The man in the turtleneck was a spiritual teacher from a Turkish lineage of whirling dervishes. His m.o. was to live somewhere with his group, stay for a while, then move on. The group's members were a typical cross-section of young 1970s American seekers. Over the months, I went to a lot of their meetings and continued to have more uncanny experiences in which events that I dreamed about would then happen to me in waking reality. Eventually, such things had happened so frequently that they no longer surprised me. I even learned that in the field of parapsychology, they had a name–precognitive experiences or precognitions.

During this period, there was another of my dreams that stood out. It involved a young guy from the East Coast who'd been traveling around with the group for quite a while. He had piercing eyes that looked right into you, but was very standoffish when anyone tried to approach him. In my dream, he and I were sitting in New York's Central Park, and he was talking intently about the nature of reality while staring at me with that penetrating gaze. When I woke up in the morning, the dream stayed with me because of how vivid and real it had seemed.

This dream came a couple of nights before the group was going to be leaving Los Angeles to move on to their next destination. They had invited me to go with them, but I declined–give up Hollywood and show business? No way! But the evening of their final L.A. meeting, I felt a real poignance. I would miss these folks. This wasn't a cult. There was no money involved, no coercion, just a bunch of people looking for answers beyond the consensus reality we're all fed in childhood.

As the meeting ended and I prepared to leave, I heard a voice call my name. I turned, and was surprised to see it was the standoffish guy. We had never even spoken before. He took a step toward me, looked at me with his piercing eyes, and said: "*Sweet dreams, Bob.*"

The room felt as if it was starting to spin. From his

knowing attitude and ironic grin, there was no doubt in my mind that he was referring to the dream I'd had a few nights before. But how could these people do that, look inside me, even into my dreams? I had no idea and at that moment was too freaked out to even care. I managed to bolt and almost ran out of the room. I never saw him or any other members of the group again.

If you're wondering what all this backstory has to do with *The First Power*, think of the standoffish guy and then of Patrick Channing, the Pentagram Killer in the movie—how he was able to enter into people and take them over. Interestingly, Jeff Kober—the actor who did such a great job playing the serial killer who returned from the dead—is now himself a teacher of Hindu mysticism.

My career had an upward arc from the late 70s on. I had a writing partner and we wrote scripts for some major talents, In the late 80s, Columbia Pictures started The Discovery Program whereby industry professionals who hadn't yet directed could get a chance to make their first professional short film. I was one of five chosen for that honor and directed *The Jogger*, a kind of homage to Spielberg's *Duel* which is about a man in a race against death with an evil supernatural driverless truck. *The Jogger* is about a man racing for his life against another jogger.

My short got a lot of attention and gave my budding directing career a boost. A meeting was scheduled with Gale Anne Hurd, producer of *The*

Terminator and wife of Jim Cameron, the film's director. I thought about what to pitch her and remembered my old story idea about the cop and the serial killer back from the dead. At the time, no story like that had ever been made. Gale liked the idea. She liked my short. I called the script *Transit*, referencing the villain's ability to move between worlds, and we set up a deal with the legendary Dawn Steele, the production head at Columbia. Gale also arranged a meeting for me with someone she thought would be great to star in the project—Michael Biehn, a terrific young actor who was one of the leads in *The Terminator*. He and I got along well. It was now clear I had found my destiny—I was going to be the next Jim Cameron! I could live with that.

Since this would be a film about the supernatural, I thought it would be good if we did some hands-on research. Because of my continuing interest in mysticism and psychic phenomena, I participated in sessions with mediums who claimed to channel spirits who would speak through the medium's voice. I suggested to Gale it might be useful to experience something like that. She was game and said she'd bring her husband Jim along. I don't remember much about the session except for one thing. The psychic, while he was in trance, was talking about reincarnation and past-life memories and then mentioned the gladiatorial shows in the ancient Roman Colosseum. I was surprised afterward to learn that just before the psychic started channeling about ancient Rome, Jim had flashes about a *gladiatorial show in the Roman Colosseum.* These types of sessions can get kind of strange. But when you think about it, it makes a weird sort of sense... that if anyone had directed massive spectacles in ancient Rome in a past life, Cameron would be the one.

Though the relationship between Gale and myself started well, eventually Hollywood's famous creative differences reared their ugly head. Differing points of approach. Script problems. I couldn't get the ending right. Disagreements led to blow-ups. This led to the project being put in turnaround.

But the project still had life in it. Melinda Jason—my then agent, now wife and the guiding angel of my entire career—set up the movie at Interscope with super producers Robert Cort and David Madden. I had worked with them before at Fox when they had given my writing partner and myself our first writing assignment. David Madden and I went on to become close friends. David had the mind of a cinema savant—after seeing a movie once, he remembered every scene in the film. Many times when I had my usual struggles with an ending, David would pluck something out of the ethers and make the script whole.

As the film's star, Lou Diamond Phillips pointed out in his insightful, articulate foreword, he and Madden had worked together on *Renegades* in 1989. I was a big fan of Lou's work in *La Bamba* and we were all thrilled when he agreed to star in our picture. As a first-time director, I was doubly blessed. I had seen friends chewed up on their first films by narcissistic stars who wanted to run the whole show. Lou was the opposite of that. Though he had much more production experience than I did, his collaborative nature and commitment were always to the film and not to his ego.

Nelson Entertainment, the company that was now financing the film, was doing it on a lower budget and this meant production changes. Originally, the script was set in New York City where Channing's character worked in the dark depths of the subways. Another of the reasons for the film's title being *Transit*. Though L.A. had its own subway lines, they didn't have the hellish underworld feeling that the film required. So we opted for L.A.'s Department of Water and Power and the subterranean world of its reservoirs. Aside from a few real locations, most of the ending was done on immense sets in the San Fernando Valley where we pumped in huge volumes of water to achieve the necessary effects.

Editing a film is an intense process. I remember the hole I felt in my stomach when we drove up to our first preview and saw the lines around the block. *What if they hate it?*! But the audience seemed to enjoy the ride and I was relieved as we approached the ending, the one part of the film I had total confidence in. Naturally, the ending bombed and we ended up in reshoots. Next came the nerve-wracking opening weekend, a highlight of which was watching from the back of the theatres as the scary moments literally had people jumping out of their seats.

As is often the case with many horror films, some of the reviews were less than kind. We got especially killed in the Los Angeles Times. A year later when the film first played on television, <u>the same reviewer</u> called it an underappreciated gem and gave a strong recommendation that people not miss it this time around. Thanks, buddy–where were you when we needed you?

The film was a surprise financial success and for Nelson Entertainment was second only to their biggest hit–*Bill and Ted's Excellent Adventure*. A nostalgic note for me was when *The First Power* played in Brighton Beach's Oceana Theatre in Brooklyn. That was the theatre where I fell in love with movies as a kid. My father who lived in Brighton Beach would hang out in front of the theatre and query the viewers coming out. "So, did you like the movie?" When people said they did, he'd just grin–"My son directed it!"

People sometimes ask me why I never directed again. It's pretty straightforward. The projects they wanted me for, I usually didn't like. The two or three I would've killed for came down to me and another director and the other guy got it. So I continued with my screenwriting career and never looked back.

At the end of the day, I'm proud of *The First Power*. It's certainly far from perfect, but the truth is it's hard to make a film about the supernatural and mystical. There are moments in the movie, however, where I think we came up to the border between physical and non-physical reality. When such moments happen in a film, our human response is to feel a chill and creepiness moving up our spines. If you have any reactions like that watching our picture, then we achieved our goal.

Since I never got to make an Oscar speech for the film, I want to use this opportunity to mention some of the talented people who worked on the movie:

JOHN MOIO – extraordinary second unit director and stunt coordinator. In his next life, John will probably be a great writer/director who will leave all of us in the dust.

MICHAEL BLOECHER – a very fine character/dialogue editor who also worked on *The Terminator*. I know I disappointed Michael by not directing again, but in our short collaboration we made some beautiful music together

THEO VAN DE SANDE – wonderful Dutch/American cinematographer who was so important to the look of the film. I think Theo must dream in Film Noir, both in black and white and color.

MYKELTI WILLIAMSON – a first-rate actor whose talents are on display in films like *Forrest Gump*. Mykelti always dreamed of being a director and I'm very glad he achieved it.

STEWART COPELAND – esteemed member of the band The Police. Stewart's accomplished everything in the music world you can possibly accomplish. Listening to his intricate, labyrinthine scores you can feel like you're hearing three scores at once.

MARILYN VANCE – Academy Award-winning costume designer. An amazing eye for detail, Marilyn could put together magnificent costumes worthy of the Royal Family out of items she bought at swap meets and the Salvation Army.

PATRICK JOHNSON - not only a talented director but the innovative creator of the knife/cross for the nun Sister Marguerite. My sincere apologies once again to Patrick that somehow his name got left off the credits!

Last but not least, many thanks to CHRISTIAN FRANCIS for his passion and excellent novelization of the film. Christian is a true lover and devotee of the horror film. If you end up going against him on *Jeopardy*, stay away from all categories having to do with cinema horror. Together, he and I came up with an ending for the novelization that I wish I could've thought up for the film. If I had, maybe I could have become the next Jim Cameron!

TERMINUS

1989. The Los Angelean skyline sprawled under a thick blanket of smog clinging to the city like mold, turning the sky a dull, morbid orange even in the dead of night. This heat had squatted over the streets for months, thickening each day, seeping into every alley. Even after the sun left, the air still pressed itself downward, syrupy and suffocating stinking of gasoline, cigarette ash, and rancid fried food. If a breeze dared to make itself known, it dragged with it the stench of the rotten trash strangling the sidewalks. This heat was everywhere, no crack in the asphalt or brickwork could escape it.

The moon shone high above, attempting to illuminate this city. But its muted glow was easily overrun by a multitude of buzzing, flickering, faded blue and pink neon signs casting weak halos over the shadowy streets and graffiti-covered walls.

This city's pulse of distant, stuttering car alarms sounded in rhythm and was only broken up by the wailing of sirens that rushed on by. There were no tourists milling around the streets. No partygoers causing drunken raucous outside the clubs. Here, a feeling of fear permeated every part of this city.

The streets, from Hollywood Boulevard to Westwood, would otherwise be a bustling hive of activity, even at this late hour. But only the desperate and the destitute braved to venture outside and those who fought to protect them.

The only cars present were police on patrol, shining their flood lamps at anything suspicious that they passed, always vigilant. Their lights passed over hookers and johns who scurried away like vermin. Or dealers who stayed huddled in their darkened corners, waiting for another junkie to stumble up, wide-eyed and desperate. Some were homeless souls wanting to sleep in their stupors, as well as those twisted by addiction and madness, who spent their days screaming to the skies about their delusions. Past all this desperate collection, the police carried on. They didn't have time to stop any petty crimes. They were patrolling the streets for something else.

The Pentagram Killer.

An all-night newsstand sat bravely open without a single customer since the city turned dark. The vendor sat on his stool, shotgun within arm's reach under the counter, slumped over the prior day's copy of the

Herald Examiner. Barely awake, he struggled to keep his eyes open.

The headline in front of him screamed "A City in Fear." These bold words lay heavy on the page in smudged black ink, stained from his sweaty hands. Underneath that, a picture of an innocent, smiling ten-year-old girl held her teddy bear for the camera. Underneath it, the caption read: *Victim #15: Alicia Morgana.*

A digital clock on the wall proudly shone 2:17 a.m. into the murky living room, and the rickety AC unit jammed in the open window hummed loudly as its fan strained to blow cool air inside.

Russell Logan sat slumped in front of an old scratched-up table as he stared down at the open notepad in front of him. He spun the pen between his fingers over and over as he tried to piece all the information together. He had little idea what time it was because he was too invested, too focused.

His black T-shirt and jeans did nothing to cool him down, and his olive-toned skin glistened with sweat in the light from the window. The street lamp shone an orange glow past the open curtains of his fourth-floor walkup. Its hue illuminated the cluttered room around him, glaring over the dozens of newspapers, open files, and crime scene photographs. Not to mention empty cans of beer and boxes of half-eaten takeout. The latest of which was a cold pizza that sat by his front door. It may have been forgotten by him, but his overweight cat, Jack, had discovered it and nudged the lid open with his head. He sat, happily chewing the cold cheese off his second slice.

The only thing Russell had found time to do in his mental zone was smoke, and the overflowing ashtray on the edge of the table was evidence of such. Each new butt he added to the pile became a game of dare against gravity, one he was winning.

Under his notepad and spread out over the table was a street map of Los Angeles. From Topanga Canyon to Hacienda Heights, the map was littered with black Xs marked at random locations. Scrawled above each was a different timestamp. On the notepad, he had scribbled down his ideas: *Revenge? Money? Hate? Love? Cult?* Each was crossed out and dismissed after some intense thought. And scrutiny.

Logan stared at the Xs. Trying to see something, *anything*, he hadn't seen before. Something to link them all together, time of day, type of neighborhood, but every possibility he investigated came to a grinding halt. He felt like the Xs were staring back, silently mocking him.

His eyes traced between each X, trying to make sense of it all.

There must be a hidden pattern.

Reaching his pen to the farthest X, he then moved it to another, connecting the points.

There must *be a hidden pattern.*

The line went to another X. And another. And another. And another.

His eyes widened as his pen slowed down.

There must be a...

He stared at the jumble of newly drawn asymmetrical lines over the map. *These lines have no pattern. No sense.*

He glanced at the pile of dog-eared books stacked at the other end of the table. Books he had read from cover to cover, hoping to find a clue. To help find the motive, to see a chink in the armor. A weakness he could manipulate to solve this puzzle. But those books on demonology, arcane symbology, cults, and mysticism did nothing except make him so much more confused.

His frustration grew.

"Dammit!" he growled as he grabbed the edge of the map, yanking it from the table before throwing it across the room.

When he cast it to the floor, along with his notepad, the overflowing ashtray spilled all over his shag-pile rug. As the glass ashtray thudded onto the wooden floorboards, Jack bolted toward the bedroom, a slice of pizza hanging from his mouth. A slice so big he had to drag it backward. The bell on his collar jingled as he scampered away with his stolen prize.

Catching this escape in his periphery, Logan couldn't help but chuckle. "Atta boy."

In his thirty-three years as a proud member of the Los Angeles Police Department, Logan had spent longer as a beat cop than most would dare. He was the cop who wanted to remain on the front lines, committed to his belief that his presence on the streets made a real difference in people's lives. For him, this wasn't only his employment but his calling. A devotion. A religion.

The neighborhoods, the people, these were his to protect. And he took great pride in knowing the rhythm of each and every block he had ever walked, every alley and corner, the faces that called these streets home. He didn't chase promotions or have any inclination to rise through the ranks, since he was happy where he was. His Filipino- Hawaiian heritage and darker complexion helped to gain the trust of neighborhoods that typically felt disconnected from the predominantly White LAPD.

However, fate had other plans. It was when he broke the Readcrest Ripper case, a brutal series of murders that had confused the department, that Logan found himself on an unexpected trajectory. When senior officers had hit dead ends and were ready to give up, Logan's street-honed instincts cracked that case wide open.

Then the top brass all but begged him to accept a promotion to homicide detective, a role he had never even considered before. He resisted at first. He liked his life on the street too much, and he wasn't convinced that wearing a new title would change anything. But practicalities loomed, he needed the bump in pay that came with the job. And so, reluctantly, he stepped into the world of homicide, figuring he'd try it out.

It wasn't long before Logan had been plunged into an abyss of human cruelty he never could have imagined before. Gone were the pastoral visits across his section of town, the domestic disputes, the low-level dealers, the prostitutes. Now the whole of L.A. was his beat, and what he witnessed was terrifying. He came face-to-face with the most depraved, who exacted their cruelest acts upon innocents. Cases that crossed lines of age, gender, race, and religion. Cases he found, despite the horrors, that he excelled at solving. He was far beyond the rest of the officers at predicting the perpetrator's next twisted steps and piecing together their motives, even if they themselves thought they did not have one. Logan could figure it out.

With each newly solved case, Logan felt a bittersweet sense of accomplishment. The city needed someone willing to face the worst to keep them safe, and though it was a role he never wanted, he had become that someone. After a few years, he could do more good by facing this dark underbelly.

So, that is what he did.

For the past sixteen years, he had been a detective sergeant, promoted after yet another serial killer was captured and incarcerated.

He sighed as he closed his eyes. The tiredness was

finally catching up with him as soon as he took his attention off the map.

The phone sprang to life as it rang. Its jarring volume cut through the silence and through Logan's thoughts with a jolt. Even Jack, happily eating his stolen pizza slice in the bedroom, jumped again at the sudden mechanical ring that echoed through the apartment.

Glancing up at the clock, Logan then turned his gaze to the insistently ringing phone sitting by the door on a short bookshelf.

"Someone better be dead," he grumbled as he got to his feet.

And someone usually was dead when he got a call. The only people who ever called him were his work, who always called on his day off.

Evil never rested, and when one case was solved, a dozen others were waiting. All as important and just as terrible.

Lazily, he lifted the receiver to his ear. "Yeah?" He gazed back at his ash-covered rug, thinking he should roll it up and throw it out.

Easier than cleaning it.

"He's different," a soft female voice said at the other end of the line, a breathy, scared voice.

"Excuse me?"

"He's different from all the others," she repeated. "You don't understand that. That's why you haven't caught him."

Logan froze. Thrown by her urgency.

"I know where he's going next," she added. "Where he is killing."

Logan was used to the cranks who came out of the woodwork when a high-profile case was in the news. Dozens of people saying it was them or that it was their neighbor. But this was the first time they had called his home number.

"Look, lady, it's two-thirty in the morning. You gotta have the wrong number."

As he was about to hang up, she blurted, stumbling over her words, "The marks are always six inches in diameter, right? The wound is always at the center. And he cuts the head off, mostly. It's still on. But always the same."

Logan paused, his mind snapping to attention. "Who is this?"

"I... I can't..."

This was not information anyone outside of the department had. When he realized that, he sighed.

"Okay, you guys think you're funny? Wait till I get in."

He expected to hear laughter. To hear people from the police precinct relent, knowing their prank was exposed. But there was nothing.

"I'm serious," she said, her voice trembling.

Maybe it isn't my colleagues.

"Who is this? How did you get my number?"

"I'll tell you where he'll kill next. You can stop it. You want that, don't you?"

If this is a prank, Logan thought, *it has gone way too far with that last comment.*

"But you have to agree to something first," she added.

"Go on," he said with an emotionless tone.

"I have only one condition. *No one* dies. And most importantly, no death penalty for him."

"That's two conditions," he replied, trying to draw her out and throw her off guard.

"I mean it," she declared with a tinge of annoyance. "I want you to promise me. If you do, you can save people. It's not much to ask."

"Who are you, the ASPCA? You make it your mission to protect animals? You think that animal, whoever it is, needs some protection? Are you his wife or something?"

An uncomfortable silence filled the void between them as static on the line fizzled in the absence of sound.

"Goodbye," she eventually said, her voice soft and dejected.

"Wait! Okay, okay, tell me what you know."

"Swear it. Swear that no one will die. Swear he won't get executed."

"Fine, you got it, no execution. No killing. Now, tell me your name."

Silence lingered again. A much longer silence.

A more uncomfortable one.

"Hello?"

"The south entrance to Elysian Park off Sunset," she whispered.

"Are you there? Do you need to meet?"

"Go there now. He will be there. He will. I can't say when. You just have to wait. But it will be when it's dark."

He couldn't stop his eyes from widening. *This has to be a prank*, right?

"Don't forget your promise, Detective Logan."

The line went dead.

He stood, holding the receiver as the disconnect tone buzzed in his ear. Slowly, he set it down, then walked over to the ash-covered map.

Shaking off the debris onto the rug below, he laid the map back on the table. Staring down at the white line demarcating Sunset Boulevard, he traced it along with his finger to the south entrance of Elysian Park. He picked up his pen and drew a new X at this location.

"This has gotta be bullshit," he said under his breath.

But as he stared at the X, something clicked. With this new mark, a pattern he hadn't noticed snapped into place.

"You gotta be kiddin' me," he said as he drew more lines over the map, much thicker ones. "Russell, you stupid asshole," he chided himself. "It's so obvious."

Standing back, he stared at the lines. The shape was an inverted pentagram with a circle surrounding it. The new X was the last link, the intersection of two lower points.

He stood, staring, heart pounding.

He *had* to call this into his team.

————

Three days later, Downtown L.A., even in the depths of the night, was a surreal blend of glamor and grit. With the lighting in the office high-rises always on, the looming buildings cast an electric glow around them. Each window was an amber or neon pinprick against the darkness of the sky. Below, a fine mist of smog hugged the streets, giving the ambient lights a hazy, seedy, dreamlike glow, as a faint shimmer from the daytime heat still radiated from the ground. Beyond these glass towers, hidden in the backstreets, were grime-coated warehouses and garbage-slicked alleys.

As the clock struck midnight, a thundercloud rumbled as the sky released a light drizzle upon the uncomfortable heat. A summer storm. Its droplets swirled down with the breeze, past the rooftops, and reflected in the corona of the street lamps.

Under a blanket of newspapers, a homeless man was stretched out on a park bench. He scowled as the raindrops got bigger, hitting down on his newspaper sheets with wet thuds.

With a crackle of static, a voice rang out from the homeless man's earpiece.

"Sleeper, check-in," it said.

The man shook his head as he adjusted his newspapers. "It's goddamn raining," he grumbled into the hidden mic attached to his lapel. "Even a sick fuck killer won't come out in this bullshit."

A few hundred meters away, a car was parked on the side of the street. Its lights and engine switched off. Through the windshield, a man could be seen in the driver's seat, leaning over a figure on the passenger side in a seemingly passionate embrace.

With a crackle of static, a voice rang in this man's earpiece. "Hey, lovebirds, you there?"

The man, moving away from the inflatable doll he had been pretending to kiss, shook his head. "No offense, boss, but this is a wild goose chase."

"Well, thanks for your expert feedback," the voice replied sarcastically. "Now, get back to it and remember to use protection."

The driver sneered, then lifted his middle finger to the glass toward the person on his earphone. The driver chuckled as he shook his head, then leaned back over the doll to mime their passion.

"Carmen?" the voice asked into the earpiece of a young woman.

Dressed in the shortest of skirts and wearing the highest of heels, she walked along the sidewalk, keeping an eye out for any signs of life.

"Nothing here," she replied under her breath, lowering her head down to her lapel mic. "No one even asked me for a date yet. It's dead around here."

"No one asked you?" the voice replied. "Well, you can always go for a drink with me after this. I can show you some fun."

"Dream on, Mazza," she said with a smirk.

On a nearby rooftop on Sunset Boulevard, overlooking the entrance to Elysian Park, Detective Albert "Mazza" Mazzaro raised a pair of binoculars to his eyes, focusing on Carmen, who walked the street below. A smirk spread across his chubby, pockmarked face as he spoke into the walkie-talkie in his other hand, barely holding back his chuckle.

"Aw, you break my heart, babe," he said, before then addressing all the undercover officers on the same radio frequency. "Now, boys and girls, keep your eyes peeled. We got a bad guy to catch."

Mazza scanned his binoculars along the street and up the building.

The rainfall stopped, the briefest of respites to the heat. But as it left, it made the air much more humid and much more uncomfortable for Mazza, who was sweating.

"You better be right about this, Logan," he mumbled as he put the binoculars down and wiped his forehead with his jacket sleeve.

Carmen made her way down the dim, deserted street. The clacking of her heels echoed around her.

She peered across the road at the entrance to Elysian Park, where a Stygian blackness swallowed the path beyond. Even the distant crest of Dodger Stadium, usually seen peering above the treetops, was masked over that night. Its lights turned off. Its presence was only a dark shadow.

A scraping then shot out from an alley behind her, making Carmen's pulse leap as she turned. Her fingers slipped into her jacket pocket and wrapped around the handle of her police-issue revolver. Taking cautious steps forward, she strained to silence her heels against the concrete below.

Clenching her jaw, she braced herself, preparing to draw at the slightest hint of danger. As she was trained to do, she edged closer to the alley's shadowy mouth, her breathing falling shallower and quieter as her muscles tensed.

A shape shot out from behind a trash can with a piercing yowl.

Carmen could not stifle her smile as she released the grip on her weapon, realizing it was only a cat.

Crouching, she extended her hand out toward it, whispering, "Hey there, you got a home, little guy?"

The cat padded over to her, but it then halted, its eyes unblinking, not at her but behind her.

"Don't be scared. I won't hurt you."

The cat's ears flattened back, and it let out a low, rasping hiss, before retreating into the darkness.

Before she could process its warning, a large hand

15

emerged from the shadows behind Carmen, clamping over her mouth, suffocating any scream. Another arm then wrapped around her neck, squeezing the air from her lungs. She struggled, kicking out desperately. Her heel then struck the trash can, sending it crashing onto the ground.

Catching the commotion, a motion-activated light then snapped on above them, casting a harsh yellow glow. Its garish beam illuminated the brutal, jagged lines of a pentagram inked into the rough skin of her attacker's hand.

She thrashed, eyes wide, as her vision clouded. Growing weaker, her body went limp.

————

"All positions clear," Mazza rang out over the police radio speaker.

Detective Oliver Franklin smirked in frustration. "Now, what did I tell you?" He turned to Russell Logan, who was sitting in the passenger seat of this unmasked sedan. "We've done days of this shit and nothin'. Tonight's no different. We gonna give it up?"

Nearly three decades younger than Logan, Franklin never held his tongue despite Logan also being his boss. They were partners, as well as good friends.

A rising star of the department, Franklin knew the city better than Logan. So much so that it was as if his

16

nervous system had been wired directly into the very rhythm of the streets. His sixth sense for cases was almost as good as Logan's. It was only a matter of time before this young detective was to be promoted to be *his* boss despite his lack of tact.

"Don't ya think we should shitcan this and go home?" Franklin continued. "Everyone's burned out."

"Yeah, well, our good friend, Mr. Pentagram, is out there," Logan replied. "And *he* isn't getting burned out, is he? It feels like he's warming up. That all this is the start of something bigger." He spoke as he peered up the empty, dark street.

"What if that woman on the phone *was* his old lady?" Franklin asked. "Setting us up? You know as well as I do how much these assholes love to play their mind games."

Logan turned, looking pensive. "Well, you didn't hear her. She sounded scared, terrified."

"She could just be a good actor."

"He'll show," Logan said, convincing himself as much as his partner. He then looked down to the crumpled map, at the scrawled pentagram linking all the dotted Xs, and whispered, "He'll show."

"Christ, man," Franklin laughed. "He'll show, he'll show. You've been saying that for days now, since she called you." Grabbing the Saint Christopher medallion from around his neck, he lifted it to his lips and kissed it before looking upward. "Saint Christopher, please protect me from this heathen evil bullshit and from all the evil shit you're throwing at us."

Logan couldn't help but grin at his partner. "You know your problem? All this mumbo jumbo occult stuff got you creeped. Same with everyone else. They look at this guy like he's the actual boogeyman. He's a person. Flesh and blood. Fallible. Just 'cause there's a pentagram doesn't mean he's the devil."

Franklin shrugged, pointing to the map. "All I know is some whack job called you on our night off, feeding your connect the dots obsession, and now... we follow that lead for days. And nothing. So, you took us off-book."

A spark of guilt flashed over Logan's face.

"Oh yeah, I *know*," Franklin continued. "Ain't no way you got this cleared for more time. And if this goes sideways, I'll probably get busted down to desk duty on the south side."

"Is that all you're worried about?"

"Isn't that enough?"

"Nancy and the kids will love it there," Logan chuckled. "Isn't the south side where *all* the upstanding folks of the African American community live? I hear they have fine cars with tinted windows, real high class and all that."

"Oh, fuck you," Franklin replied, trying to hold back his grin.

"That's 'Fuck you, sir'!" Logan commanded with a cheeky grin.

"I swear, if you were white, I'd be allowed to punch you in the dick for that!"

Two patrol cars sped through the intersection with flashing lights and wailing sirens, then screamed to a skidding stop ahead.

"Fuck," Logan said. "That's the commander."

"Guess I'm going to the south side, then," Franklin muttered mournfully as he slowed the car down.

Getting out of the lead patrol car, Commander Alan Perkins, sixties, bald, gaunt, and perpetually stressed, turned as Franklin and Logan's sedan pulled up beside them.

From the other side, Lieutenant Jonah Grimes emerged, a tall, red-faced man with the nose of a chronic drinker.

Logan got out before the engine was turned off and strode over to the lieutenant. "What the hell is this? This is a stakeout, not a damn parade."

"Is that what you call it, Logan?" Grimes asked with a sneer. "Seems more like a jerkoff."

Logan turned to Perkins, hoping for some backup.

"You asked for twenty-four hours," Perkins said, shaking his head. "That ended two nights ago. We gave you the chance. Nothing happened. And you've been wasting resources chasing this lead."

"Please, Commander," Logan said, stepping around the patrol car to him. "I said I wasn't sure when this would go down. But the location lines up. You saw the map. The pentagram. And my informant says that is where he is gonna strike next."

Grimes sneered as he chuckled. "Right, yeah, this mystery informant that called your house. Did she have a crystal ball to tell you this absolute horseshit?"

"Lay off, Grimes," Perkins sighed, exhausted by everything. "Russell, I can't take the risk anymore. The department is spread too thin as it is. We got eighteen men sitting out here when this guy could as easily hit the Westside or the Hills." He smiled weakly to elicit sympathy for his words. "If that happens, can you even imagine what the media would do to us? To all of us? Not to mention all the other crimes we got going on."

"Logan doesn't care," Grimes said, waving his hand. "He cares about getting his face out there. He will ruin this department so he can be The Almighty Russell Logan as he bags his fourth serial killer. Film at eleven!"

"Sixth," Logan corrected. "Anyway, it's good to see you out here, Lieutenant. Guess all the bars must be closed—"

"Russell," Perkins said, trying to calm this tension.

Anger boiled in Grimes as he stared daggers at Logan before turning to Perkins and saying through gritted teeth, "Commander, I don't know what you see in this jumped-up prick, but I went on record saying that this stakeout would be a colossal waste of resources, and it would go nowhere. Just because he was in the right place at the right time for a few cases doesn't make him a fucking hero we should bend over for. He ignored your order and did this for forty-eight hours longer than was authorized. That cannot go unpunished." He turned back to Logan. "Look at you, jeans and a T-shirt? You don't even dress like a detective. You look like a goddamn street punk."

With a steely stare, Logan took a threatening step toward Grimes, but Perkins grabbed his arm to pull him back.

"*Russell*," Perkins chided. "Both of you, stop acting like damn children."

"Where the hell are you, Carmen?" Mazza mumbled. He held the binoculars in both hands as he scanned the street below him. "Dammit." He grabbed the walkie talkie from the wall beside him. "Walker... come in Walker."

No answer.

"Walker? Carmen? Do you read me?"

Panic rose from the pit of his stomach, like a vat of acid waiting to overflow.

Still sitting in the sedan, Franklin could only watch as Logan argued with Lieutenant Grimes and Commander Perkins.

"Walker MIA," Mazza sounded over the police radio. "I repeat, Walker MIA."

Logan was almost losing his temper with Lieutenant Grimes, but before any more insults could be tossed around, Franklin called from out of the sedan's window, "They lost Carmen! Parkside, north of Sunset."

Without saying another word, Logan bolted to the car.

"It's all bullshit," Grimes grumbled to Perkins. "You know it is. She's off taking a piss or something."

Perkins peered at Grimes, unimpressed.

An urgent jam of police cars was crisscrossed on the other side of the street, their lights flashing as Logan and Franklin pulled up in their sedan.

Logan raced ahead over to two uniformed officers, who were sweeping their flashlight beams across the alley behind a toppled trash can.

"What've we got?" Logan asked, his gaze darting around the scene.

One officer gestured to a series of scuff marks across the pavement. "These weren't here during the last patrol." He shrugged. "Looks like something went down here. Or we didn't see the marks before?"

Examining the marks, Logan instinctively could tell they had been caused by a struggle. Following the trail along the sidewalk, they halted at the edge of the curb. "He must have taken her in a car."

"Dunno how. Sunset's blocked in both directions," Franklin said. "If he was in a car, which way could he go?"

Logan's eyes shifted around the area, checking for side streets or alleyways. His gaze then landed on the shadowy entrance to Elysian Park.

Through the darkness, the police sedan drove slowly behind Logan with its high beams on. He walked ahead cautiously, gun in hand, as he peered around. His expression was determined as he forced all anxiety aside.

He's only a man, Logan repeated in his head.

Ahead, the shadows parted as they found themselves at the large metal gate that led into the south side of the park.

The glare from the sedan's headlights shone over the thick chain locking the gates shut but hung down limply, having been cut.

Noticing this, Logan's excitement rose alongside his dread.

Without a second to think, he pushed open the gates of the park and carried on.

Amid the urban sprawl that made up the City of Angels, Elysian Park stood as an anomaly north of Chinatown. With its rolling hills, verdant trees, and expansive green landscapes, it betrayed the mass of concrete and glass that surrounded it. A natural beauty nestled within the heart of a man-made monstrosity, Elysian Park spanned over six hundred acres, a maze of hills and woods, with snaking hiking trails throughout.

As night lay over the cityscape, the park was calm. Occasional raccoons scampered across its moonlit open lawns and glens. Here and there, the faint glow from the city lights peeked through gaps in the foliage, barely illuminating the dirt paths that wound deeper into the park's heart.

An old pavilion bandstand stood on the eastern lawn, but instead of being masked in darkness, a yellowish glow emanated from within it.

Etched by small candles tracing the outline of her body, Carmen lay naked and unconscious in the middle of the bandstand. Her hands and feet were bound by rope and tied to the fencing encircling her. Her limbs were splayed out, and a gag covered her mouth.

A large figure, wearing a long black hooded coat, stood beside her, looking down. A large knife hung in its sheath from his belt underneath.

He then circled her, lighting the remaining candles around her body. This figure's actions were calm.

As he lit the last candle, she came to. The ache in her head pounded and her heartbeat sped up as she realized where she was. Her eyes widened in terror as her mind adjusted to this scene. Between her bare body, being tied up, and what the man was doing, she could only focus on the large knife hanging from his belt.

The figure's lips parted as he chanted, "Lux obscura tenebris, flammas evocat in perpetuum."

She tried to scream, but the cloth covering her mouth muffled the sound. She then flailed her legs and arms, but the binding made it difficult to move. As she screamed more, her eyes filled with petrified fury, and she begged in grunts to him.

Meanwhile, he paid her fear and anger zero attention, focused only on her body as he muttered his incantation. "Corpus et spiritus in tenebris offerimus, ut potentia inferna augeatur."

He drew his serrated knife from its sheath and crouched over her bare abdomen.

As he held the blade high above himself, moments passed, and he stayed in this position. Blade held high as he mumbled his chant over and over again.

An abandoned '76 Mustang stood on the grass verge in the Elysian Park parking lot. Its doors had been left wide open. Behind it, the sedan pulled up with a skid.

Darting out, Franklin grabbed his flashlight and shined it inside the open muscle car, a revolver firmly in his other hand. But there was nothing except the empty seats.

"Nothin'," he called out as Logan searched around the car.

He, too, held a revolver at the ready.

Noticing a patch of grass to the right of them had been dug up from something being dragged on it, Logan called, "You there!"

With their lights and guns out, both rushed from the car onto the grass. As Franklin broke into a run, leading the charge, Logan followed, his flashlight beams disturbing the grooves in the dark lawn beneath him, conscious of his surroundings, always pointing his gun ahead.

The lawn soon turned into an incline where a bank of pitch-black trees shrouded the top of a hill, separating them from the eastern lawn.

The blade traced over Carmen's naked belly as the hooded figure continued to mumble in Latin.

Through the trees, the two detectives raced frantically in pitch blackness. Their flashlights' thin beams highlighted their path as much as they could, but the shadows here were thick. No moonlight had found its way down through the knotted branches above.

Logan, still leading, had lost the tracks he had followed. The scraping through the grass dissipated the further into the tree line.

"He must've carried her," Franklin said from behind. "Can't see shit at all out here."

A few feet ahead, the tree line broke as the moon could finally light their way. As they stepped out, the ground fell into a steep slope, down onto the eastern lawn. Logan slowed his pace down the incline. Franklin, though, had no time, losing his footing as he hit the grass. He tumbled forward down the grassy knoll with an uncontrollable yell, his flashlight falling from his grasp.

The cry in the distance cut the Latin words falling from the figure's lips. With his knife still over Carmen, he looked up and out across the dark lawn.

Carmen, her eyes closed in terror, did not hear Franklin. She prayed as tears flowed down her cheeks.

Without a sound, the figure retreated backward, past the pile of sliced clothes cut from Carmen, and into the shadows on the far side of the bandstand.

"Carm!" Franklin called out as she got to the surrounding fence, seeing her tied-up, splayed body. He scanned around with his gun and torch, making sure no one else was around, before calling out behind him, "Logan! Over here."

Carmen could not speak, but her eyes screamed for him to run. Franklin did not notice her silent pleas, nor did he see the fist that came out of the darkness toward him.

The pentagram-scarred hand flashed out and smashed into the side of Franklin's head with a terrifying force. The blow of which sent his body crumpling to the ground.

The figure was then on Franklin's unconscious body, knife raised, ready to kill.

"LAPD. Freeze!" Logan shouted as he approached the bandstand hurriedly, a glowing beacon in the middle of the park's darkness.

He could not clearly see the attacking figure, Carmen, or Franklin, as they were all obscured by the surrounding fence. But as he placed his foot on the first step, the figure had turned on him.

Before Logan could fire, the figure's long, hooded coat billowed out like a shroud as he leaped toward him. It slammed into his chest and sent them both crashing backward off the structure and onto the lawn.

The wind was forced out of Logan's lungs as he collided with the ground, the figure's weight fully on top of him. As his grip broke free from his gun and torch, they both fell onto the grass.

Logan had little time to think. Stunned and wheezing, he rolled free from under the figure as the serrated blade pierced the darkness and slammed into the dirt, missing his head by mere inches.

His mind was running on pure panicked instinct. He only knew he had to get out from under him.

Desperately, he then lifted his leg and kneed his attacker hard in the groin, sending him reeling back. Logan rolled out and grabbed hold of his fallen gun, turned it on the figure, and fired.

No warning. No arrest. Only bullets.

Bang.

Bang.

Bang.

Three shots.

But the figure did not stop as he staggered away across the lawn, disappearing into the night. Injured but able to move. His long coat flapped out behind him as he ran.

Scrambling to his feet, Logan peered back into the pavilion and saw Franklin, dazed and bleeding from a head wound, hurrying over to Carmen.

"You okay?" Logan shouted, gun held up and ready as he looked out to where the figure retreated.

"We're good," Franklin replied as he winced in the throbbing pain from his wound. "Go get him!"

Without missing a beat, Logan set off and bolted across the lawn. With his gun in hand, he didn't waste more time looking for his fallen flashlight. He couldn't let the man get away.

He sped over the rising and falling landscape ahead of him, ignoring the pains in his lungs as he struggled to control his breathing.

A sudden sound from the underbrush to his left, of branches breaking, caused Logan to turn and then run toward it without thinking. His aim was leading his way through the moonlight.

Ahead of him, as he passed through the breaking of trees, the figure's billowing coat caught Logan's attention before the figure suddenly picked up unnatural, immense speed. Sprinting away much faster than Logan could run.

Coming out of a tree line and down onto one of the surrounding streets, Logan had lost track of his quarry. He looked both ways down the street lamp-lit asphalt, but there was nothing around him. Not even parked cars.

He tried to catch his breath and had to bend over, feeling the burn in his lungs. His smoking habit, as well as his middle age, meant that his condition was far from where it was when he first joined the force.

As he turned his gaze downward, he caught sight of a few drops of red liquid on the gray concrete curb in front of him.

Blood?

Logan couldn't hide his smirk. One of his shots had hit its target.

Squinting to see through the dull streetlight, Logan traced the fallen red dots across the street. They led up to an alley between two large industrial warehouses. Large brick buildings, ominous in their size.

Cautiously, he stepped through the darkness, trying not to give away his position. He moved over the strewn filth that overflowed from nearby dumpsters. Attacked by the local wildlife looking for food, the trash had lined the whole alley's width with waste and rot.

His gun still aimed ahead, Logan kept to the left side of the alley that contained the most shadowed cover, hugging the wall as much as possible. As he got farther into the down, he noticed a low metal sliding door on the warehouse, left wide open.

He peered at the ground in front of it, where the moonlight shone over a couple of droplets of blood leading inside.

Inside the vast two-story high space, faint moonlight trickled in through the grime-coated windows high up. The building looked abandoned in the shadows, with its large metal machines placed around like ancient monoliths.

All sound within this cavernous expanse reverberated. Drips of water from one of the broken pipes provided a rhythmic backbeat as occasional haunting creaks from the building sounded from far above.

Logan, wishing he had spent the extra second to pick up his flashlight, crept along, wondering where in there the figure was lying in wait.

Then the sudden sound of shuffling caused Logan to turn and fire.

The deafening shot rang out as the bullet thudded into the brick of a nearby wall.

"Piggy, piggy," a malevolent voice said with a laugh from somewhere in the room. "How many shots ya got left, piggy? Two at most, I'd say. Maybe less."

Logan turned his gun to his left, his wide eyes struggling to focus on where the voice was coming from. But in this space, the sound reflected off from every wall and surface.

Another horrible laugh, this time echoed from his right side. He turned his aim, following his line of sight.

Nothing.

Stepping across the warehouse floor, Logan gripped his aim tighter as he got to the base of a metal staircase.

As he moved up, he kept his gaze concentrated as he looked over the warehouse beneath him, using his higher vantage point as best he could. Looking around each machine below to see the figure, but the shadows were too thick.

Another giggle reverberated, but this time, he could tell it came from ahead, up on the next floor.

Stealing his resolve, Logan crept up the metal steps.

Up on the second floor, a collection of huge printing presses stood high before Logan as he stepped in through a wide doorframe.

Before he could even search the area, a shuffling of feet to his right made him whirl his aim around. The moonlight through the windows caught the silhouette of the man against a press. But before Logan could react, the figure dipped sideways, slithering into the darkness.

"Could have got me there, piggy," the figure uttered gleefully, voice still implacable.

Logan's expression was alert as he stepped forward to the press. Gun held high.

Without time to turn, a large, heavy metal paint can came hurtling out of the darkness and slammed into Logan's arms, catching him by surprise. His body crumpled to one side. Gripping his revolver tighter, Logan darted across the open space, down the back of one of the presses.

Using these rows of machines around him as cover, he let his revolver lead the way. Tracking through each shadow as calmly and methodically as he could.

But then a screech from above made Logan glance up in time to see a towering pile of metal printing plates slide off from the top of the press, teetering dangerously before tumbling toward him.

He stumbled backward, narrowly avoiding this avalanche of aluminum and steel, as it crashed onto the floorboards in front of him with a thunderous, echoing cacophony. The impact rattled around the room, sending tremors through the air.

A flash of movement ahead then caught Logan's aim in time to see the figure, silhouetted against a window, standing directly in front of him. The large knife in his hand glimmered in the light.

Without a pause, Logan fired a shot.

The figure dodged to one side as the bullet missed, pinging off a nearby printing press and fracturing a window.

With a frustrated grimace, Logan strode forward over the fallen plates, keeping his aim as he followed the figure's movements.

He pulled the trigger.

Click.

No more bullets.

A giggle from the advancing figure was cut short as Logan dropped his gun and rushed forward as fast as he could.

Logan barreled into the figure with a furious cry. As he wrapped his arms around the figure's large bulk, he pushed him as hard as he could toward the cracked window.

Locked in a deathly embrace, Logan and the figure

smashed out of the industrial warehouse's second-story window. Their entwined bodies plummeted down onto a large growth of bushes beneath.

Though their impact was not deadly, the sheer force threw them apart.

Logan roared in pain as his shoulder dislocated and ankle twisted. But he had no time to react before the figure sprang up and straddled him, pinning him down onto the grass.

In his swift movement, the figure's hood slipped back, exposing his face fully under the harsh glow of the street lamps. His features were sharp and unnaturally angular, almost feline. His eyes burned with a savage intensity, with irises dark as coal. An unhinged, cruel grin spread across his face as he took in Logan's pain. This figure's shoulder-length loose hair, wild and dark, fell around his face. Tendril-like strands framed his expression that only intensified a feral look.

In a swift and brutal movement, the figure slammed his large blade into Logan's side, slicing through his flesh and muscle with terrifying ease.

He then ripped the blade out as fast as it went in and stabbed again.

Then *again*.

Logan did not stay still. In a fury of pain and panic, he elbowed the figure's hand off the knife and reached up, grabbing the man by the throat. Digging his fingers in as hard as he could. Logan had an equally murderous look in his eyes.

Despite the blood pouring out from the open wound in his midsection and the knife embedded in his flesh, Logan pulled at the figure's throat, forcing him down, off the grass, and onto the street.

Like a man possessed, Logan had turned the tables and scrambled on top of the figure. Letting go of his windpipe, Logan grabbed the figure's head and smashed it into the asphalt.

The figure had no time to fight back as his skull collided with the road.

And Logan couldn't stop himself. Through his gritted teeth, insurmountable agony, and intense fury, he bashed the man's head in again and again. But despite this, the man smiled at him as his head was repeatedly smacked into the solid ground. Wearing that same grin, the man lost consciousness, and his body went limp.

Logan, though, didn't have any care to stop. He kept smashing the man's head into the ground. With each wet thud, he cried out in rage. As the blood seeped out from a wound on the man's head and into Logan's fingers, he just kept going.

He didn't hear the sirens as they approached.

He didn't even hear the policeman running over to him.

He could only feel his fury as he, too, began to lose consciousness.

JUDGMENT

"It's Over," the bold newspaper headline read, sat over a collection of pictures of smiling faces.

The victims of the Pentagram Killer. Young, old, Black, White, male, female, American, tourist. Fifteen faces smiling out of the page in a collection of high school photos or candid home shots. The only thing linking these victims was the fact that they were in the wrong place at the wrong time.

For the people of the city, it felt like a weight had been lifted. They milled around, smiling at each other, being polite. Happy that the danger had left the streets.

"All day, we've been covering the conclusion of a months-long operation by an LAPD special task force, led by Lieutenant Jonah Grimes, which, last night, successfully brought the notorious Pentagram Killer to justice. Once again, the City of Angels can breathe a sigh of relief," Felicity Kernawicz said with a beaming smile into the camera.

Her heavily made-up face and overly teased blonde hair were a familiar mainstay on local people's televisions. As coanchor of KCBS News at 6 Los Angeles, she was used to talking of tragedies over the recent months, but the news was far from sad.

For the past twelve hours, every news station had been flooded with reports of the Pentagram Killer.

The screen changed to a black-and-white picture of Logan sitting up in a hospital bed surrounded by Franklin, Mazza, and Carmen smiling at the camera.

"We can report that the task force's lead officer, Detective Sergeant Russell Logan, has been taken off the critical list after his dramatic battle in the early hours of the morning."

The screen flicked back to Felicity, who was still smiling. "This is the third time in nine years, and the sixth over an illustrious two-decade career, that Logan has been responsible for the death or capture of a serial killer. Not to mention the countless rapists, child abusers, and other high-profile criminals he has brought to justice. We at KCBS News send Detective Sergeant Logan our thanks. You are our guardian and deserve every medal the city has. We now go to Brad Withers, who is in Blanchard Canyon in Tujunga. Brad?"

The screen shifted to footage of an older man dressed in a blue plaid suit, holding a microphone and speaking into the camera. Behind him lay a small shack. Uniformed police officers and plain-clothed detectives left the shack one after the other, then loaded boxes of collected evidence into police trucks.

"Thank you, Felicity," Brad said, addressing the camera. "I am here in the hills overlooking the quiet neighborhood of Tujunga, where, unbeknownst to the residents, Patrick Channing, the man who we now know as the Pentagram Killer, lived. Behind me, Channing's workshop. And you can see the many police here, who are now collecting evidence."

A work photo of the angular-faced man, with shoulder-length black hair and dark, blank eyes, appeared in one corner of the screen. Below it scrolled the words, *Patrick Channing. The Pentagram Killer.*

"Coworkers described Channing, an employee of the California Water division, as quiet, solitary, good at his job. No one we have been able to speak to has any clue that he would be capable of the atrocities that we now know him responsible for."

The news reports carried on like this for weeks. Spinning the same information in a myriad of different ways. Interviewing people who knew Channing. Trying to find out an answer to why any of it happened. Trying to make sense of this terrible summer. But most of all, trying to be as sensationalist as possible to get the ratings, promising revelations, but only offering repackaged information.

———

Six weeks later, it was no different.

The news report flickered with images of a gauntlet of police officers that stood in line outside the Clark County Justice Courts. News camera panned across the scene, capturing officers attempting to manage a large crowd of reporters and onlookers who stood, waiting. Many held protest signs. *Death to Channing, Kill the Killer, Justice for the 15*, as well as many other scrawled slogans.

"Demands for the death penalty have intensified in the Patrick Channing Pentagram Killer case," the reporter narrated over images of the murmuring crowd. "In a controversial move, the trial was transferred to Nevada from California, where the death penalty is not an option, an intentional decision by the LAPD to ensure the maximum punishment could be pursued. A move approved by Channing's own legal team. Channing has already said he would plead guilty to all fifteen counts of murder in the first degree. He has stated that he feels no remorse and is happy with his actions, that he, and I quote, 'committed these acts with full knowledge of what I was doing. I was not coerced and should not be given any leniency. I ask the good people of the court to make sure that justice is done.'"

The screen then cut to a car pulling up outside the courthouse. From the driver's seat, Logan got out. With a stick in his hand, he walked with a hobble up the court steps.

"Detective Logan?" the offscreen reporter said, thrusting his microphone among the many others begging for a sound bite. "Detective Logan, do you really want Channing to get the death penalty?"

Hesitating for the barest fraction, Logan then turned to the reporter with a smirk. "You better believe I do."

This sound bite would be replayed over and over for the next few hours. A gift to reporters.

Another reporter asked, "What about those who say that the move of the case to another state could be seen as an illegal violation of Channing's rights?"

"Hey, he agreed to this," Logan said. "Not like we dragged him to Nevada against his will."

"And what about critics of capital punishment who say that this reduces us to the same level as those we punish?"

Logan paused with a serious look straight into the camera. "That's an important question. There's only one proper answer." With a defiant gleam in his eye, he leaned in close to the microphone, puffed up his cheeks, and let out a long, noisy raspberry, the vibration of his lips echoing his disdain.

The people listening roared with approving laughter as another vehicle then pulled up a few feet away.

"It's Channing!" one person shouted.

"He's here!" screamed another.

Logan chose this moment to continue up the steps, the reporters having moved on to the man of the hour.

From the large armored police van, flanked by a dozen armed police officers, Patrick Channing stepped out. Manacled. He was then led from the van, through the crowd, and up the steps of the courthouse. Wearing sunglasses, Channing grinned widely. Loving every second of this.

Through the line of policemen, Logan stood at the top, waiting for Channing to be escorted.

"Hey, how's it going, Russ?" Channing asked with a laugh as he spotted Logan ahead of him.

"Going great." Logan smirked. "Almost didn't recognize you without my fist in your face."

Lifting his hand to the armed escort, Logan motioned for them to stop as he continued to talk to their prisoner.

"You didn't recognize me?" Channing mocked, feigning disappointment. "But my picture's been plastered over every TV screen and newspaper for weeks. You must have been in a really shitty hospital. Speaking of which, how's your stomach? I see you got a stick now. Cool accessory. So, for that, you're welcome. Let me know if you need another."

"One will do, pal," Logan replied, taking his weight off the cane. "In case you get out of line, I can beat you with it."

"That's *swell*," Channing said. Though he was

smiling, his eyes were fixed on Logan like a shark hunting its prey. "I hope you can do me a favor and have a word with the judge?" Before Logan could answer, Channing continued. "Don't let those pussies fink out on me. I mean, if a twisted piece of shit like me doesn't deserve the big one, then who the hell does, right?"

Russell shrugged. "You realize you could've saved us all the trouble and done it yourself years ago?"

"But then I would never have got to have a dance with you, my friend." His face turned serious as he leaned in. "Pity I couldn't finish, eh? Anyway, promise me. Have a word, make sure that they *really* punish me."

"Right on. Will do," Logan replied politely.

"I knew I could count on you, Russ." Channing winked at him. "I owe you one."

"Bring him through," a voice rang out from inside.

With that, the guards led blankly through the court door.

As they did, he shot a glance back at Logan. "See ya round, buddy boy."

"I doubt that," Logan murmured.

As sunset approached and the distant L.A. skyline came into his view, Logan drove down the I-15. He looked at the city through his windshield, to the orange hue of smog, and felt somewhat better. He always hated to leave his hometown. Especially when he didn't feel well. An ache throbbed in the pit of his stomach from an annoying side effect of the raft of medications he had to take. Various opioids, anti-inflammatories, and blood thinners, to name a few.

Promise me you'll take it easy for the next few months, the doctor had said to him. *Your injury is quite significant, so you need to rest as much as possible. Lie down. No work. No driving. No lifting. If it involves moving your torso, please, for your sake, don't do it.*

Logan remembered those words clearly. He wasn't ignoring them out of spite or ignorance that he somehow knew better than a man who studied medicine his whole life. Some things were more important than his immediate recovery, and he *would* rest. He just had to see Channing at the court. That was the period he needed to put at the end of this terrible chapter of the job. The end of a saga he had to see to its completion. To deliver the perpetrator to justice.

He had no intention of watching the trial, no intention of giving Patrick Channing another iota of his attention. He had done his job, caught the killer, and seen him to court, injury or not. It was justice's turn to do what it was supposed to do. He didn't want to waste his time watching a second of what would happen. What Logan presumed would be an elongated cry for an insanity plea. He was done and needed to drive home. Then he could rest.

But the burning in his stomach was a reminder that he was not doing well, that his healing from such a violent injury would not be a fun experience. There would be no superhuman feat of recovery. It would be a painful hardship.

You can expect to feel a few side effects from the meds, the doctor had advised. *Stomach cramps are the primary side effects that you should expect. We'll prescribe some painkillers for that as well, but despite taking those, you may still feel at least mild discomfort in your gut. The other common side effects are nausea, constipation, itching, dizziness, dry mouth, all the way to auditory and visual hallucinations, severe depression, and chronic paranoia. Opioids can be dangerous if taken incorrectly, as all medications can be. So, no taking more than you should, and if you have any problems, call us twenty-four seven. Understood?*

The side effects the doctor had told him were the bare minimum. Logan had dared to read the warnings on each bottle of pills he had been given, the terrifying effects they could cause. Whether antibiotics, painkillers, or analgesics, all listed the veritable banquet of horrors he could probably experience. But he was experiencing cramps in his abdomen. Cramps he couldn't calm with alcohol, he had tried. Food didn't even help. Nothing did.

He just had to ride them out by ignoring them. So, he did what he always did to take his mind off things. Worked. Of course, he would take it easy, as the doctor suggested, by working at his office desk, until the pain got to be too much.

———

Less than a week later, the news channels were filled with an immediately iconic image of Patrick Channing. Sitting in the court with a blank expression. A chilling stare into nothingness. He had been branded a monster, but with that picture, they called him everything from the devil to death itself.

The court case had run for over a week. It had heard testimonies from experts detailing the terrible crimes committed. From prosecutors presenting all their evidence in meticulous detail to forensic examiners going through all the belongings they had found at Channing's house, blood samples of victims they found on his unwashed clothes. Dozens of books on the occult which Channing had highlighted various passages in. Not to mention the diaries that Channing had written, describing in extreme detail exactly what he had done to each of the bodies. The symbols he had carved into each of their remains, alongside corroborating crime scene photos of each. One after the other, this procession of grotesqueries went. A watertight case was presented to the twelve men and women of the jury.

All while Channing stared emotionlessly and blankly ahead with very shallow breaths.

When it came time for his defense, the court-appointed lawyer had not objected to a single statement from the prosecution's case and spent the whole time sitting quietly next to Channing. Standing, they picked up a piece of paper from the desk and read out a simple statement.

"It is my client's wish that this court and the good people of the jury know that he, Patrick Channing, committed these crimes of his free will and with careful planning. He is not insane. He merely wanted to kill them, so that is what he did. Would he kill again if released? Most definitely. If incarcerated, would he kill again? Most definitely. He has no plans to lie to you, and with that in mind, the defense rests and will not be presenting any arguments on behalf of Mr. Channing."

The papers and television ran wild with this story. It was perfect fodder for them to glamorize for the news cycle before the verdict was due to be read out a few days later.

———

Logan did not spend the week at work as he had planned. Instead, he had spent it in a hospital bed, having blown out his stitches from the exertion of the drive to and from Nevada. When he arrived home that night, he noticed blood had seeped through the dressing on his abdomen and through his gray shirt.

It was then the pain got worse. Much worse.

Spending that night in hospital, in a burning agony,

the doctors increased all his medications and gave him even sterner warnings.

"I don't think you understand, Mr. Logan. You nearly *died*. Simply put, you did." The doctor did not mince words as he visited his bedside. "And you've got to take care of yourself. *Please*. Or your body will not have time to heal, and you'll risk everything from infection to a lot worse. You can die from this. So, we're increasing your medication, and for at least the next few days, we will administer a sedative. And you'll stay in this bed for that whole time. Do you understand me?"

He did. But Logan didn't like it. He had no choice, though.

The next five days were spent in a haze. Between ghoulish nightmares that plagued his medicated sleep to waking to hallucinations brought on by the cocktail of opioids flooding his system, Logan mercifully felt little pain. He only felt the fear.

Every nightmare played out the same. *That* night. *That* chase. *That* warehouse. *That* high fall. *That* large serrated blade splitting through his guts, slicing through flesh and organ with a disturbing ease. Over and over and over again. All the while, Channing bared down on him with an enormous grin, giggling incessantly.

Then, each time when he woke, it was equally terrifying.

The muted television on the wall opposite him was

always on. But when Logan sluggishly came to from a replaying nightmare in his mind, he saw every person as Patrick Channing. A news reporter talking about climate change was him. The weatherman. All of them. Same face but as if from another reality. When the news ended and was followed by an episode of some insipid family sitcom, every character that appeared on screen was *also* Channing. The kids, the parents, the grandparents, the famous guest star. Whether female or male, young or old. All had his face. And when he turned up the volume, they, too, had Channing's voice, Channing's laugh.

He would then be fed by a nurse, all while he saw her with the killer's face. Saying things that any nurse would say. Same for when anyone came to visit. But they were all Channing, too.

Logan knew he was hallucinating. He just had to ride it out and not rise to it. But every single moment filled him with an intense, primal fear. One that made him unable to do more than just exist.

His world in the hospital was a sludgy daze, as he repeated this cycle of the nightmare, hallucination, nightmare, hallucination, day after day.

On the fifth day, the doctor lessened the sedation, and over the next eight hours, the hallucinations faded. The leering image of Patrick Channing on everyone's faces gave way to the real people in front of him and the real people on television.

"I think we're through the worst of it, Mr. Logan,"

the doctor said. "You seem to be healing perfectly well. I think with a couple more weeks of rest at home, you should be okay to resume light duties again. But you cannot push yourself. Just be patient. You still have a lot of medications doing the hard work for you, and you cannot drive, okay? You are not fit to operate any machinery."

Logan was sitting at home on Monday morning, reading a book in his dressing gown, when a cooking show in the background was interrupted, piquing his attention.

"We bring you a KNBC special news bulletin," the newscaster said in a sensationalist manner. "The Pentagram Killer, Patrick Channing, was, this morning, found guilty on all fifteen counts of murder in the first degree and two counts of attempted murder."

When Logan heard this, he could not help the satisfied grin edging its way up his lips.

The newscaster continued. "The presiding judge, the honorable Alan Thicket, in a landmark ruling, sentenced Channing to death, marking the end of a trial that has gripped the nation. Crowds gathered outside the courthouse, celebrating what they called 'justice served,' while few condemned the death sentence as excessive."

Logan was surprised Channing was telling the truth all along. This *is* what he wanted.

The image on the screen then changed to one of Channing in the courtroom with a huge grin. "Judge

Thicket concluded the sentencing with a firm statement, underscoring the severity of the crimes and the court's commitment to a swift and decisive resolution. He ordered the sentence be carried out at the Nevada State Prison in Carson City within the next seven days, in what some are calling a 'highly unusual measure.'"

Logan grabbed the television remote and then quickly changed the channel.

Feeling somewhat better, Logan agreed to go into the precinct the next day to celebrate with his colleagues. A move the doctor would not have advised but one that Logan felt he had to do. Not for himself, but for his friends. For Carmen, who desperately needed closure on what happened.

Unlike him, her injuries were not physical but left an indelible mark on her. A mark everyone in homicide understood. They arranged the gathering to celebrate the nightmare being over. Something she needed more than anyone and something that had to have been on hold while Logan recuperated. He knew this, and going into the office by taxi, showing his face and having one drink was the least he could do.

When he walked into the precinct with his cane by his side, looking quite weak as he hobbled, Logan was met with a loud cheer. From desk clerk to sergeant, everyone congratulated him, as it was the first time he had been seen by most since that night.

He smiled as humbly as he could. He loved yet also hated this attention.

"Hey there, brother," Franklin shouted out as Logan limped into the homicide department, face pained as he moved.

Above Franklin, a large banner said *Congratulations* in glittery letters, as bottles of champagne lined the long desk below it, with a few empty glasses sitting nearby.

The whole department was there. Each with a glass already in their hand. Every one of them looked happy and relieved.

"You really playing the long con with that stick, eh?" Mazza chuckled as he handed Logan a glass of champagne.

Logan looked very hurt by the comment.

Franklin wrapped his arm over his shoulder, staring at Mazza sternly. "Dude. No. Not funny."

"I didn't mean..." Mazza stuttered. Looking horrified that his jest may have offended, he stared at Logan, wide-eyed. "I'm so sorry, Russ."

Logan took the glass from Mazza. Then, with a sudden smile, he dropped his walking stick to the floor, stood up straight, and laughed. "Gotcha!" He pointed at Mazza.

Mazza couldn't contain his laughter. "Oh, you beautiful bastard!"

"And that is why he is the boss," Franklin added, dropping his fake act of annoyance.

"You should have seen him," Carmen added as she walked over, happy to see her boss. "I saw him out of the window. You hobbled in from the damn taxi. Now that's some method shit!"

"Hiya, Carm," Logan said as they hugged.

"Well, I for one am impressed," Mazza said, adopting an English accent. "I doff my cap to you, good sir."

Despite Logan's happy exterior, he was over-playing his health. Standing straight was painful, and his side ached despite the sedation he had taken. But that night, he would show none of that. He couldn't allow Channing to be seen as having any effect on them after that day. So, he ignored the pain, ignored the bright colors that pulsed in the periphery of his vision. As he would try to act normal, he would wait to go home to feel the lingering pain and medicated side effects. Monday, after all, would bring in a whole new slew of cases. New bad guys to catch.

"Uh, boss," a junior detective called from the other side of the office. "You got a phone call over here."

"Bet that's the commissioner wanting to give you a blow job," Franklin said.

Logan shook his head and smiled, walking across the office to the phone. "I wouldn't take it if he offered, not after last time."

Mazza turned to Franklin quizzically, mumbling, "Think he's getting a promotion?"

"Oh, without a doubt," Franklin laughed.

"Yeah?" Logan said, lifting the phone to his ear.

Behind him, the office buzzed with celebratory chatter.

"You *lied* to me," the female voice said.

Her tone was more hurt than angry.

"Excuse me?" Logan strained to hear over the noise. "Can you speak up? I can't hear you."

"You promise no death penalty."

Logan's expression dropped. He had forgotten about this woman. Her demands. Her intel that led to Channing's capture. Through the trial and ruling, no one had even stopped to follow up on her. His injuries and the celebration took over everything.

"Stop it before it's too late!" she added. "You only have a few days!"

"Hey—"

The woman had hung up.

Frustrated, Logan replaced the handset and turned back to join the party. He would have to find out who she was and how she knew.

––––––––

The execution was scheduled to take place on the following Saturday at 5 p.m. Five days after the sentencing.

In the bullpen's history, the colloquial term for the Nevada State Prison in Carson City, Nevada, there had been sixty executions. The execution of Patrick Channing would be the last, number sixty-one, before the bullpen would begin to close. From there, Ely State Prison would then assume control of all its inmates. From the aging infrastructure and limited capacity, the bullpen was a dinosaur that had been left to ruin for decades. The peeling, cracked walls were only the most obvious signs of its dilapidation.

In its gas chamber, deep in the prison's heart, where the first execution by lethal gas on American soil happened sixty-five years earlier, a large gray wooden chair sat. Splintered and high-backed, the chair was as worn as the rest of the prison, except for the fact this chair had had sixty men die in it. A fact that made looking at it that much more disturbing.

Around the chair, at the bottom of the plain surrounding concrete walls, small dirty vents led to the sulfuric gas canisters.

In front, a large, thick glass led to an observation gallery. Even that glass was not clean, nothing here seemed well maintained. In the gallery, fit for twenty people, were spaces for the nine witnesses required by law and another eleven who wished to witness.

When it was time for the execution of Patrick Channing, witnesses were chiefs of police, mayors of Los Angeles and Carson City, local politicians, and Detective Sergeant Russell Logan. All sat in the darkened gallery, looking into the overly bright gas chamber. It was macabre, like a theater audience about to watch a play.

Logan had not wanted to be there. He found no joy

or satisfaction in seeing what was about to happen. He had argued against it a few days earlier when he was asked by Commander Perkins. But the Carson City mayor had insisted that the arresting officer be present. Something that the LAPD were all too happy to agree to without consulting Logan.

As he sat on the far end of the front row of chairs, Logan stared through the glass at the empty execution chair. Its straps lolled open to the concrete floor. He shuffled in his seat as his stomach wound twinged in its familiar dull ache. As he swallowed, his spittle tasted metallic, like blood, *another* common side effect he had not gotten used to.

He glanced at the other witnesses. *Could that woman who tipped us off be here as well?*

The door to the chamber opened and the man of the hour was led in. Manacled by his hands and feet and dressed in a gray prison jumpsuit, Channing was hauntingly calm. He showed no signs of any resistance and appeared somewhat content. As he walked in, he calmly sat in the chair. His expression was pleasant as he politely offered his hands up for the chains to be removed by the prison guard.

The guards strapped him into the chair with its large, thick leather restraints. Torso, arms, and legs all held in place, and as they were, Channing looked pleased with himself. Various electrodes were then placed over his body to track his vital signs. From them, wires snaked into a junction box on the far wall.

"Hey," Channing said to the guard with a cocky grin as he motioned to his arm. "Left one's a little loose. Might wanna check that."

But these guards were not playing around. They did not engage with him as they stepped aside.

Channing turned his stare into the darkened observation room ahead of him. His grin did not waver for a second. One by one, he stared at each person's shadowed face until he got to the end of the row, to Logan, and then his smile somehow got even bigger.

At that moment, a guard lowered a hood over Channing's head.

But Logan could still sense his grin. Even if it was blocked, he felt like somehow Channing was still staring at him, despite the thick fabric.

As the door to the chamber closed, with the guards all having left. A loud clank of the bolts locking rang out.

This was it.

This was the last moments of the life of Patrick Channing. And from the sound of his muffled laugh, he could not be happier.

A few silent moments passed where nothing happened.

At the far end of the observation room, an older man in a black suit stood in front of a bank of monitors. Each displayed Channing's pulse and other vitals, such as air pressure, oxygen balance, et cetera.

Channing tapped on the arms of his chair as he

waited impatiently for what was about to happen. "Who's dick I gotta suck to be killed around here?"

Then a loud hiss filled the room.

As a thick white cloud formed and billowed upwards in the small chamber, Channing's chest rose and sank as he took the largest, deepest breaths that he could.

His body then jerked. Spasming violently against his restraints. His back arched outward as his muscles contorted.

The cloud around the chair grew denser until the witness's view of the twisting body of Channing was fully shrouded.

Five slow minutes passed. Five uncomfortable minutes. Witnesses stared at the thick cloud, knowing what was happening within.

Logan didn't feel an ounce of relief. He felt nothing except the ache in his side and the sickness in his stomach.

A mechanical buzzing then sounded, followed by a loud hiss. The thick white cloud was soon sucked out of the room, dragged back through the vents as it was replaced by clean air. As it cleared, Channing's body came into view, slumped in the chair.

The man in front of the monitors, with a maudlin expression, respectful to the occasion, turned from the flatlining readings and calmly said, "It's over."

With a collective sigh of relief, the witness gallery

stood up to leave, when one of them gasped in horror, staring into the gas chamber.

In the chair, one of Channing's arms twitched.

"Just some aftershocks," a guard at the back of the room said. "Like a chicken without a head. Happens all the time."

They all stared at the chair with a mix of shock, horror, and fascination. All except Logan, who rubbed his eyes from exhaustion.

The colors he had hallucinated in his vision before were back. Filling the chamber in front of him with a kaleidoscope of vividness. They pulsed in waves with his heartbeat on the edge of his vision.

I need to sleep.

He tried to shake it off. To will it away.

Channing's arm twitched again.

"What the hell's going on?" the Carson City mayor demanded.

Then the impossible happened.

A scream roared from an old man in the gallery as Channing's arm ripped upward, tearing through the leather restraint like it was made of paper. His other arm surged upward, the buckle on the strap breaking open under the force.

Then his legs kicked out, breaking free with as much ease.

His body then lunged forward as his bindings tore off.

He was no longer tied down.

The scream was followed by a few more. People in the gallery backed away toward the door, confused and scared.

Logan sat, staring wide-eyed at what was happening. Wavering slightly. Feeling a sudden wave of nausea.

Is this real? Am I asleep? Is this another nightmare? Or another hallucination?

Standing with the hood over his face, Channing ran blindly toward the observation room window and, in a furious flurry of punches, battered the thickened glass as hard as he could.

By the door, the guard, not able to see the full extent of what was happening, said, "Please, everyone, calm down." He held his palms up to them. "We will handle this. Everything is fine—"

Glass of the execution chamber shattered, as Channing's bloodied fist broke through it.

With a roar of rage, he launched himself at the glass and forced his head into the small expanding crack. The sharp edges sliced through his hood as he pushed inward, ripping into the fabric and then through his terrifying, grinning face. Cutting through his flesh, he squeezed his head inward, cracking the glass further. The shards sliced into his flesh and tore it back, exposing the bone beneath as the blood gushed out.

Logan, still in a confused daze, got to his feet and backed away from the fury that shredded its own face to pull itself through to the observation room. His mind spun as his vision tilted and turned. His stomach contracted as a new pain shot through his body, causing him to grip his side and yelp in agony.

At the window, blood gushed from Channing's wounds, and he clawed his way through to the gallery. The lacerations across his head and body were deep and had skinned off most of the flesh on his face, exposing his teeth and the side of his pale jawbone. But none of it seemed to affect him.

"Let us out!" screamed one witness.

But the guard at the door could not move. He was so transfixed in fear as the heavily mutilated yet grinning monster stood in front of them.

The other guard in the room pulled his gun and was trying to aim at Channing, but the witness pooling in his way didn't give him a single clear shot.

"Move!" the guard shouted.

But no one was listening.

Channing, still grinning, with blood spilling out of him as his skin hung in shreds over his head, then turned to Logan.

Trying to focus through his spinning, colorful vision, Logan opened his jacket and reached for his revolver, keeping his eye contact with Channing.

In Logan's mind, the colors danced around as Channing took a step closer to him. The floor shifted beneath them from left to right as if on a pendulum, but the monster kept walking.

Logan shakily raised his gun, trying to focus.

Bang. He fired a shot. Straight into Channing's skull.

Bang. Another shot, but this time into Channing's heart.

With a terrifying laugh, totally unaffected, Channing reached inside his prison grays and pulled out a long-serrated knife. The same knife Logan had been stabbed with.

He then roared as he ran at Logan, the knife held high.

Logan was too afraid and confused to move as he closed his eyes, trying to stop the colorful horror that advanced at him.

Then an unearthly howl erupted.

REGRESSION

An unearthly howl erupted.

Jack, the fat, short-haired black cat, howled again as it jumped off from the windowsill and onto Logan's chest.

With a jolt and a gasp, Logan woke up from a deep and terrifying nightmare. Covered in sweat, his breath was ragged as he glanced around the room, making sure the world was right again.

As he sat up, a wave of agony burned from under the bandage on his stomach. He ignored it as he wiped the sweat off his forehead with one hand.

Jack howled again, this time following it up with a purr as he rubbed against Logan's arm.

"Yeah, yeah," Logan said, regaining his faculties as he scratched Jack behind the ear. "I'll get you some breakfast."

Swinging his legs off the bed, Logan stiffly and

painfully stood. Peering down at the floor where he would normally do his early morning push-ups. He then recalled the doctor's orders: no exercise for three months.

Noticing Jack staring up at him, Logan smiled. "I'm not gonna, okay? So, you can stop judging me."

Checking the bedside clock, 8:08 a.m, he already felt a sinking feeling of dread.

It was Saturday, and he had to go pick up his mother from her church. He had been delaying going to see her since she came to the hospital and made a scene by screaming at the doctors.

"This is Satan's work!" she shrieked at the doctor as he tried to give Logan a tetanus vaccine. *"You're insulting God's pure designs by jamming that filth in his veins!"*

Logan was glad to get out of the hospital, primarily to stop feeling embarrassed by what his mother had done on each visit. The doctors, of course, were understanding after she left, but Logan still felt ashamed of her views. A far cry from his own.

He was raised in the strictest of Christian households, and since leaving at sixteen, his spiritual beliefs were at zero. As he once told Franklin, he could never tell his mother he was an atheist, as she would probably have him kidnapped and fed an IV of holy water.

Franklin found that hilarious. Logan, though, would not put such an extreme, ludicrous thing past her. This was a woman who bathed him in bleach after she caught him masturbating when he was ten. She was... devout. And that day, he had to see her. All he wanted to do was to figure out who the woman who tipped him off was, a question that kept repeating in his mind, gnawing at him.

Rosario Luzviminda Logan. Born in 1914 on the island of Cebu in the Philippines, she brought her faith with her when she moved to America. Since the day she had left her home, she had felt more of a need to bask in the pages of her chosen holy scriptures. Moreso, she felt America was a country rife with sin. And one she felt needed a lot of prayer to fix, for her, but even more for her son, Russell.

Wearing all black, Rosario sat on her couch, watching the television as she held her hands in her lap. At seventy-nine, she looked every bit as strong as someone half her age. She was not a person to reckon with, and Logan rarely did. In fact, to get her to leave the hospital, he had to pretend to be asleep for over three hours until she caught the last bus home, all done instead of confronting her.

"Is the food okay, Russell?" she asked, gaze glued to the television.

A game show played out quietly in front of her.

Logan sat at the small dinette table behind her, eating a large plate of pot roast, mashed potatoes, and peas. Expertly cooked, as always. But it was one of the three meals that she always cooked, not that Logan was complaining. The food always outweighed the sermons he would invariably be subjected to when seeing his mother.

"Great as always, Ma," Logan replied with a half-full mouth.

Rosario shook her head and sighed. "I think I over-cooked it tonight."

Logan chuckled to himself. Of course his mother would never accept a compliment as being true. Pride was a sin, after all.

"Well, I'm telling you it's great."

Her eyes never left the television's glare, her expression hardly changing as she spoke in a monot-one. "You could have come into the church today. Father Russo really wants to meet you. I told him all about you, and he's seen you in the papers. He thinks you could benefit from what he could teach you."

"Ma, can we leave saving my soul till after I eat?" Logan said before shoveling a large piece of beef into his mouth.

Turning, Rosario shook her head at him with a rueful expression.

As the television switched from game show to game show, it soon played out banal sixties sitcoms. And when it did, the volume was turned up. The canned laughter echoed around Rosario's house.

After the dinner, Logan and his mother sat in the living room watching television together. Logan wished for the time to pass so he could leave.

Eventually, she fell asleep and began to softly snore.

In the electric glow that filled the room, a large painting of Jesus on the wall in front of Logan stared back. As if playing a game, Logan stared back. As he did this, he did not notice his mother wake up and stare at him with concern.

"Russell?" she eventually said, voice trembling.

Breaking away from his staring, Logan turned to his mother. He took a beat as his stomach dropped. *Here we go*, he thought as he gritted his teeth.

"Yeah, Ma?"

She looked shaken.

"Hey, Ma," he added preemptively, trying to swerve the conversation. "I better leave you to sleep. I feel a bit—"

"You were dead."

Logan looked confused.

"I was all alone because you had died." Rosario's voice sounded strange against the backdrop of the sitcom's laughter. "You *left* me alone."

"In your dream?" he asked, trying to mask his disdain.

"And your immortal soul was in the lake of hell because you had killed," she whimpered as tears rolled down her cheeks. "And God said thou shalt not kill! He was so angry with you as you never repented."

Despite his fractured feelings for his mother, a pang of guilt twinged at seeing her cry.

Moving over next to her, he took her hands in his. "Just a dream, Ma. I'm not going to hell. You can be sure of that."

But his mother only got more upset. "It's your father's blood!" She pulled out a hankie from her sleeve and wiped her eyes. "No one in my family had that kind of anger like you both do."

Logan considered how to reply but was at a loss.

"I light a candle for you every day. Did you know that?"

He did. She mentioned it all the time.

"I worry so much about you."

"It's late," Logan said. "Come on, I'll help you up to bed."

As he got into his car, he looked at his watch. It was 8:42 p.m., late for his mother, but he had drinks to get to, for that night was not any other night. That night marked one week after Carson County Prison had filled the execution room with a lethal gas and the life of Patrick Channing had been taken away in punishment.

Getting behind the wheel, he winced. He knew he shouldn't have been driving yet, and it was the first day he had since going to the courthouse, but his mother would not have played nice in a taxi. Sure, it may have been ill-advised for his recovery, but to Logan, his mother telling the taxi driver how he was a sinner for some innocuous reason was more dangerous. It was the path of least resistance, the entirety of their relationship.

Still in pain, still in a medication brain fog, still having his vision flooded with hallucinated colors and shapes, Logan tried to carry on as best he could. The medication course would be over in a month. He had to make it till then, hide any effects.

At least he had got out of having to witness Channing's execution. After the persistent nightmares about it, he could not ever sit in that observation room. And his commander was more than happy to tell the Carson County Mayor that Logan's health mattered more than any photo op he had in mind.

Tonight was all about trying to regain normality by going out for drinks with colleagues. Colleagues who needed to move on.

"To the ones who didn't get away," Franklin said, raising his glass of beer high.

Sitting in a booth on the mezzanine of Neon Nights, a club that tried way too hard to be cool and, with its dive bar roots, came off as too seedy to be fashionable. Franklin sat opposite Logan, speaking over the pounding music that boomed up from the strobe-filled dance floor below them.

Logan clinked his glass with Franklin's. He was feeling exceptionally cotton-mouthed and fuzzy from the painkillers. He ignored the residual ache in his side, as well as the imagined colors bleeding into his vision.

"Dude," Franklin added with a huge grin. "You got stuck in the guts three times. *Three* fucking times! And look at you! Any other person would be still in hospital grasping onto their sweet life. You, though?" He laughed. "*You* are walking about as if nothin' happened! That's some grade-A superhero shit, right there."

Logan shrugged as he took a sip of his drink. His happy demeanor masked his discomfort. From the periphery of his vision, snaking tendrils of neon danced as the sounds seemed to get louder and louder around him. But he persisted and sipped again.

"It doesn't get any better than this, boss!" Franklin added, noticing Logan was slightly off. His expression may have seemed content, and his eyes were maudlin. "Tonight, when people go to sleep," Franklin said, waxing lyrical, "there's one less creep that won't be back on the street. No time off for good behavior. No appeals, because that asshole is dead. Dead meat." He leaned over the table. "For once on this screwed-up job, we made a goddamn difference."

"I can't argue with that," Logan replied.

"Party time!" Franklin declared as a waitress sidled over to the table with six shot glasses on a tray. "Thank you, m'lady. Amazing service as always."

Logan spoke over the music to her. "Can you get six shots for the booth over there?" He pointed to the other side of the mezzanine, where Carmen and Mazza were having drinks in their booth.

The waitress nodded, then walked away.

When she was gone, Logan grabbed one shot glass and sank it in a second. Then another. The liquid pleasantly burned as it went down.

"This is supposed to be a celebration, Russ," Franklin said, taking a shot of his own. "How about taking your time?"

After downing a third, Logan smirked as his gaze drifted to a woman in a skintight black dress who wore a yellow rose in her hair, dancing against the mezzanine's balustrade. She stared back. As he looked at her, Logan could not help but think of the woman who had tipped them off.

"Hey!" Franklin said, pulling Logan's attention back to him. "What is it? You're distracted as all hell."

"Who was she? I can't get past it."

"That one on the phone," Franklin rolled his eyes. "Your mystery woman?"

"Not one lead on her. That's strange, right?" Logan motioned to the passing waitress for another round. "It's buggin' the hell out of me."

"Who cares? She could be a damn Avon lady for all it matters." Franklin laughed. "Or his masseuse. His ass wiper. None of it matters. It's over. He's dead. Job done."

Logan's gaze drifted back to the woman with a rose in her hair, who was still gazing at him seductively and gyrating to the rhythm booming around them.

"Look, he got to me, too," Franklin said. "Been seven days since they put him down. But every time I close my eyes, I still see that prick. Those eyes... And you got it so much worse. As did Carm. The dude wasn't just sick. He was evil. But, and this is the most important part, he is *gone*. Over. Finished. Kaput."

The woman by the balustrade kept her stare on Logan, and he stared back. Her movements seemed to slow the music down as she swayed.

"You gotta get him out of your head. Sure, he redecorated your insides, but you need to move on." Franklin pulled out his wallet from his jacket pocket and slipped a photo out of a woman with two young children, happy and smiling, his wife and kids. "This keeps you sane!" He pointed at the picture. "This is what you need."

Logan glanced at the photo, then back to Franklin. "Sure didn't when I tried it."

"Alice was only one person!"

Hearing his ex's name made Logan tense. It was a messy three years and an even messier breakup. And not one he wanted to repeat.

"You gotta try again, not cut your dick off in protest that the last woman you were with was a piece of shit."

Logan wanted to argue, but Franklin had a point.

"Otherwise, "Franklin shrugged as he put his wallet away, "all you'll have in your wallet is pictures of your fat, ugly ass cat."

"I'm gonna tell Jack you said that," Logan chuckled.

"Another sign you gotta change your ways. You're a guy who talks to his cat like it's his therapist," Franklin stepped in front of Logan's view of the woman, "then picks up random women for one-night hookups."

"What are you talking about?"

"Oh, so if I turn around, there won't be a woman stood there staring back at you?"

Turning, Franklin saw the woman, waved, then turned back to Logan. "You are so damn predictable, Russ!" He laughed.

Logan just nodded.

The waitress then returned with another flight of shots.

Franklin didn't wait for her to go before continuing. "Pussy's all well and good, but you've been banging so many stewardesses they should put you in the frequent flyers club. Or check you for every STD under the sun. This place is hardly health central."

The waitress paused, staring at Franklin, seemingly annoyed.

"Present company excluded," he said with a cheeky grin.

With no reaction in reply, the waitress smiled politely at Logan before walking away.

Franklin looked shocked. "Wait, I said you could have STDs, and she smiles at you?! That's cold."

"Look, I get what you're saying," Logan said. "I really do. But you're sounding like my mother."

"Hey, Russ," Carmen shouted as she appeared at the table, an empty shot glass in hand, closely followed by Mazza. "Thanks for the drinks! I'm off home now. Gonna drive before I drink too much."

"Come on, Carm," Mazza slurred behind her. "The night's still young. We got plenty of time to boogie."

Rolling her eyes, Carmen turned to him. "I told you like a hundred times already, Maz. My man's waiting up for me."

"Tell him you got a better offer," Mazza said as he shuffled from side to side in a drunken dance. An embarrassing sight for a man his age, still dressed in his worn tweed jacket from work.

Carmen shook her head. "See ya all on Monday."

"Hey, Carm, wait a sec," Logan said as he pulled out a small leather wallet from his pocket.

Carmen turned back and saw him open it. Inside was a gold LAPD shield. A detective's shield.

"Russ, you amazing bastard!" she exclaimed.

"Detective Carmen Marin," he said proudly. "But I'm also sorry to be the one to tell you that you can't have an affair with Mazza. I know, I know. You are heartbroken. And if you both weren't detectives on the same team, it'd be different."

"Aw, dude!" Mazza slurred in mock annoyance.

"I don't make the rules." Logan smiled.

"And I was just about to jump your bones, Maz," Carmen added.

"Well then, I guess I'll have to go home to my wife. Hope you're all happy!" Mazza looked jokingly annoyed as Carmen grabbed his sleeve.

"I'll call you a cab. Come on," she said.

Mazza nodded and waved goodbye to Logan and Franklin. "See ya on the flip-flop!" he shouted as he stumbled down the mezzanine steps.

"I'm not being funny," Franklin said quietly to Logan. "But they definitely are, right? Like they protest *too* much."

"Oh, one-hundred percent."

They laughed as they each lifted another shot.

Logan drank two of his in quick succession.

"And what about you, man?" Franklin said. "When are you gonna take the lieutenant's exam?"

Logan laughed. "Sit behind a desk? Die of hemorrhoids?" He shook his head as he then downed his last shot. "Not my style."

"Wouldn't be the worst thing in the world, would it? What are you, about sixty now? You gotta remember that freak almost got you! Now's the time to reevaluate your priorities. You need to quit the streets and kick back for a while. Ride a desk and let the checks roll in as you do the bare minimum."

"A. Sixty? Fuck you. And B. You're right he did

almost get me," Logan said. "*Almost*." He then grabbed Franklin's last shot and swigged it.

"Oh, you are a mighty a-hole!"

"You know?" Logan said as he glanced at the twelve empty shot glasses and two empty beer glasses. "Service is for shit around here."

Franklin shook his head, too amused to be angry, too angry to be amused. "You know your real problem?"

"Nope, but I'm sure you're gonna tell me."

"You may not like it, but deep inside, you think the whole of Los Angeles would fall into the ocean if you weren't working the streets."

"You mean it wouldn't?" Logan laughed as he stood from the booth. "But right now, I think I'm gonna call it a night." He winked at Franklin, then walked over to the woman by the balustrade.

Franklin sighed as he watched him go. "Party of one it is," he said quietly as he looked around for a waitress.

Logan did not know if it was the drink or the medication, but his whole body felt like it was made of rubber. Lights in the venue came alive, transforming the bass into a multitude of colors and shapes around him.

The pain in his side was increasing from his exertion. He resolved to take some more painkillers when he went to the bathroom.

———

The morning sun broke through the half-closed curtains into Logan's bedroom. Jack happily sat on the top of the chest of drawers. Curled in the beam of sunlight, he purred away in sleep.

Over the next thirty minutes, the sun crossed over the drawer and across a desk covered with old photos. Images of Logan as a boy with his father standing next to a 1958 Plymouth Fury and one of his LAPD graduation photos. The light then moved over the carpet, glistening inside an empty bottle of scotch and up the side of the bed to the pillow, upon which a single yellow rose lay. Next to it, a small handwritten note: 834-5778. *Francis. Call Me xxx.*

Opening his eyes, Logan felt a terrible agony not only from his handover but also radiating from his wound. With a grimace and a pained sigh, he glanced down and saw blood had seeped through the bandage in the night.

"Dammit," he seethed as he reached for his painkillers.

An empty bottle.

Holding the cylindrical bottle, he stared at it. He wondered how many he had taken the night before. He couldn't even remember leaving the club. But he *did* remember some things from later. Some things he felt the pain was worth.

With a pained smirk, he looked down to his side, at

the rose, then the note on the pillow. Without even reading it, he grabbed them both, scrunched them up, then cast them into his trash can.

A noise caught his attention. A scraping noise from elsewhere in the apartment.

This noise also woke Jack as he peered up from his sleep toward the bedroom door.

Was she still here? he thought as he checked the clock.

It was 8:43 a.m.

No. He remembered her getting up to leave at around 6 a.m.

Another scrape.

Jack jumped onto the bed with a worried hiss.

With the pain in his side, coupled with the spinning of his hangover, Logan tried to focus his thoughts.

He stepped off the bed, then grabbed his pistol from the holster that had been draped over a nearby chair, as had the rest of his clothes.

Wearing only a pair of boxers, he cautiously walked to the bedroom door.

Turning to Jack and seeing how scared the cat looked, Logan could tell he wasn't being paranoid. If it was a normal part of the symphony of noises in this old building, then Jack would have barely stirred.

No, this was *something*.

Quietly opening the bedroom door, Logan then stepped into the hallway.

Another scraping from the room ahead. The bathroom.

Raising his gun, he slowed his pace even more, edging his way to the open door.

The bathroom was empty. The window had been left wide open. And from outside, a breeze drifted in and moved the shower stall door back and forth. Its hinges scratched and squeaked.

A sudden thud from the bedroom behind him as Jack nosily ran from the bed and curled around his ankles.

"Getting jumpy in your old age, eh, pal?" Logan said. "Guess I am, too."

The ache in his side pulsed, causing his vision to momentarily blur. Staggering into the bathroom, he braced himself on the sink as he stared into the mirror. His reflection shimmered in front of him, like it was made of rippling water.

"Fuck." He exhaled as he peered down at his bandage and pulled it outward, looking inside at the wound. The blood was no longer flowing. "Gotta stop, Russ," he said as he looked in the mirror. "Gotta take it easy."

Annoyed with himself, he closed his eyes, trying to force the pain away. He would get more pills later. But he must have *something* that would help.

Opening the cabinet, he scanned it for any painkillers. But all he saw was a half can of deodorant and some indigestion tablets.

"*No, please, no!*" a woman screamed from another room.

Logan whirled around as he raised his gun in shock. Jack bolted from the bathroom and back to the bedroom.

Poking his head into the hallway, Logan aimed his gun ahead of him.

"Help me!" the woman shrieked in terror again.

The second bedroom.

Walking faster, Logan moved down the hallway and kicked open the half-open bedroom door. Advancing inside as if he were on duty and this was a suspect's house, his aim zipped around the room in a blur, checking all corners for someone.

But as he moved, his aim faltered, as what was on the wall stole his attention.

No one was in this room, but each one of the four walls dripped with a thick, deep-red viscera.

Blood.

Thick blood forming the shape of pentagrams. Of all shapes and sizes littering each surface in a horrifying, surreal way.

In an instant, his head began to ring as his vision shifted. The shapes on the walls bled heavier as the red glowed. It was as if the walls were flesh and the blood had come from inside of them. Its redness dripped down.

Slowly, he backed out and hit the corridor wall as

he stared. Then the glowing from the room dulled as the bloody pentagrams stopped dripping.

He squeezed his eyes shut as hard as he could. "Get a grip. Please get a grip."

Opening his eyes again, he stared ahead into the second bedroom. The pentagrams remained, though not glowing or bleeding.

It was then the acrid stench of copper and rot hit his nostrils, as if his mind had managed to block it out until that moment.

The loud series of thumping on the front door startled Logan, causing him to duck in defense. A sweat broke out over his body as the sickness rose in the pit of his stomach. Whether caused by his wound, the hangover, or this gruesome sight, each feeling was unwelcome.

Another thump at the door.

"Detective Logan?" came the voice. "Are you there, sir?"

Rushing over, Logan opened the door, where two uniformed officers were staring back at him.

"Are you okay?" the elder officer asked, pointing to Logan's bandages, which were sodden with blood.

"I... I'm fine," Logan replied.

"We need you to come with us, sir," the younger officer said. "Commander Perkins has been trying to reach you—"

"We got orders to escort you ASAP."

"They'll have to wait," Logan dismissed as he

turned back down the hallway. "I need you to call in for techs here right away to swab for evidence."

"What's going on?" the older officer asked as he peered into the apartment.

Logan did not look back as he replied, "There's a fucking bloodbath in my bedroom!"

Smelling the powerful stench of scotch and cigarettes that permeated through the apartment, the two officers stood in the second bedroom. They glanced at each other, unsure of what to say.

Logan, with bloodshot eyes and his wound still bleeding from under the bandage, stared around the blank walls with a look of a man possessed.

There were no pentagrams here anymore. No blood at all.

"I... I..."

He couldn't find the words.

The younger officer got the courage to speak up. "We really need you to come with us, sir."

Turning in a daze, Logan walked out of the bedroom, shaking his head. "Can you give me five minutes?"

It must have been the medication. He took too much. He *must* have.

Fifteen minutes turned to thirty as Logan stood in the shower, cleaning the blood off his wound. He held back the cries of pain from the officers, who sat in his kitchen. Then, wrapping the wound, Logan counted it as a minor victory that the bleeding had stopped, and he felt a bit better.

After getting dressed, he called in a repeat prescription for his painkillers. Claiming to have lost his bottle. Resolving to himself that he would only take what he needed and not have a repeat of the previous night.

———

The midday sun painted the city in orange as Logan drove his Buick down Sunset Boulevard and into the entrance to Elysian Park.

When the officers told him where they were to take him, he grabbed his car keys, knowing that whatever was waiting for him was not good. He did not want to rely on rides from other people, especially two officers who were looking at him like he was crazy. He wasn't crazy, he was... recovering. At least, he hoped it was that.

Images of the bloody pentagrams played in his mind over and over as he drove.

In the daylight, Elysian Park was a beautiful place. No longer shrouded in a sinister darkness, it was bright. The track leading around to the east lawn was clear so much so that he could almost drive right up to the bandstand.

As he pulled up, Logan stared at himself in his

rearview mirror and noticed his bloodshot eyes, five o'clock shadow, and unbrushed hair.

He looked like a hot mess. At least he had a shower and didn't smell of the sex he had the night before. At least he *hoped* he didn't.

Getting out of his car, he glanced around at the dozens of police officers standing around the band-stand. Each looked pale and sickened. Unlike the blank resignation they would normally wear at a crime scene, this was different. This was something that truly upset them.

Hurrying over, Franklin shook his head with tears in his eyes, looking ready to cry or throw up. "It's bad, man." He took a deep breath and met Logan's gaze. "It's *really* bad. I..."

He could not finish his sentence.

Logan noticed Mazza standing by the bandstand. A look of helplessness was etched on his face. Tears uncontrollably streamed down his cheeks.

"No," Logan whispered.

As his stomach lurched as a horrible realization crept over him, he pushed by Franklin and rushed over to the bandstand. He hoped to any God that may be listening that he was wrong.

Walking past the forensic examiners, he gasped in horror as he saw the body on the wooden floor. Tied up and splayed out in front of him. Naked. Surrounded by a ring of burned candles.

It was Carmen.

Her throat had not only been cut, but her head had been severed down to the spinal cord. Her head lolled to one side as the wound opened wide like a large bloody mouth. In the pale skin of her abdomen, carved deeply, was a pentagram. Blood had spread from her neck over the entire wooden floor, coloring almost every inch.

Her eyes, dead and blank, stared up at Logan as he stared back and felt cold rage.

Franklin stepped up beside him. "Mazza last saw her leave the club," he said, sounding hollow. "Her boyfriend said she never returned home."

"How much of that is fact?" Logan asked with no emotion in his voice, unable to break free from staring into Carmen's dead eyes.

"Cab driver confirmed picking Mazza up. Valet confirmed she got her car and drove off."

"And the boyfriend?"

"You don't think—"

"You know we can't presume. He could have guessed something was up between her and Maz? Got jealous?"

"They got her mom staying with them." Franklin shrugged. "She was waiting at home for Carm, too. Kinda rules out the husband."

Logan felt the nausea wave returning as he turned and walked off the bandstand, Franklin following. When on the grass, he spoke in a low, determined tone. "We'll track her from the time she left the club. Sweep the whole area between here and there. Every side street, every inch, got it?"

Franklin nodded.

Logan then glanced over to Mazza, who was inconsolable, as an officer led him away from this crime scene.

"We're gonna fry whoever did this," Logan continued to Franklin as he pictured what he had witnessed. "I swear to God, the devil, and every other fucker up there."

———

A Porsche 911's tires screeched as it burned rubber through the narrow corridor of an underground car park. Speeding to the lower level, the car then snaked around the corners, looking for a free spot among the packed aisles.

As it passed a one-way section, the driver saw that, down the far end, a Honda had found a space and had begun to maneuver into it.

The Porsche, though, had no time to wait. The driver slammed on the accelerator, forcing the car down the one-way aisle, honking its horn to declare the urgency. But despite its speed, despite its intent, the Porsche had to slam on the brake as the Honda calmly backed into the free space.

The Porsche driver, a stock trader, looked incensed as he punched the horn in a fury. He believed his need was the only one that held any importance, yet he had been put in his place by a Honda held together with rust.

In annoyance, the Porsche sped off angrily on the hunt for another space.

Tess Seaton, in her late thirties, stepped out of the Honda, looking shaken. She wore a pencil skirt that hugged her slim legs with a matching blazer. Her hair was cut to a neat bob, and she wore very little makeup.

She would not have been as brave to battle the Porsche if she had seen it coming. Her parking there was not a show of defiance but one of ignorance. She was deep in her own world. Buried in her own worries.

Taking a second to steady herself, she glanced around to make sure the Porsche was not coming back. Since she arrived in this car park, she had felt off. Like she was running at seventy percent, with the other thirty being a sudden, distracting nausea. But this was a nausea she was very much familiar with. She knew exactly what was happening and why she felt it. There was nothing she could do to stop it.

Around the car park, many people were milling about. Their conversations were low, broken only by the occasional cry of a child. Some were paying for their tickets at the machines, some getting their families in their cars to drive away. It was a busy time down there.

Locking up her car, Tess hurriedly walked over to the stairwell, avoiding eye contact with anyone she passed. She dreaded what was about to happen in public. She was embarrassed.

Her low heels clicked on the concrete.

Click.

Clack.

Click.

Clack.

Then it stopped. The sound beneath her feet made a wet splash, like she had stepped into a puddle, but there was no water beneath her foot.

Her heart raced as her nausea increased.

Looking down a second time, she gasped, as lapping around her leather shoes was a pool of dark-red liquid.

Lights around her then dimmed as the ambience of chattering people faded to a deep, claustrophobic hum.

Tess held her breath for a second as she closed her eyes, dreading what was happening yet not surprised. Lately, though, when this happened, it was not fun but terrifying.

She looked around, as all the people in this underground space had vanished. The only things down here with her were the cars. But also something else. Across every vehicle and up every wall in sight, blood had been smeared everywhere. As if it had all been crudely painted over by a child with too much red paint.

Behind her, the door leading to the stairwell creaked as it was yanked open, causing Tess to scream in terror as she saw him. There, standing backlit in the light from beyond his frame, a large male hooded figure loomed over her.

As he took a step nearer, Tess screamed again as she backed away. The blood coating the floor got deeper as she staggered back, the red splashing up on her ankles.

Turning, she went to run to her car, but as she did, her surroundings transformed into a large empty space, where all the cars were gone. Only the deepening pool of blood lay ahead, as the small amount of life left down here began to flicker.

Glancing back over her shoulder, the hooded figure had disappeared, and only the light from the doorway beckoningly remained.

Desperately, she turned back to rush toward it.

As she got within a couple of meters, from under the shallow water in front of her, the large, hooded figure burst upward. As if from another world, this shape appeared out of the millimeters of bloody water as if it were a deep pool.

With the large serrated knife, he reached out for her.

She had nowhere to go.

The figure had her in his murderous grasp.

She screamed as if it was the only thing left in her world.

"Watch out, miss," an old man shouted as he grabbed Tess by the arm, yanking her backward.

As he did, a car sped by along the aisle, missing Tess by inches.

Shaken and almost hyperventilating, Tess realized where she was and was about to blindly step into the path of death.

With her scream still resounding around the car park, Tess looked around. All the cars were back, not even a single drop of blood in sight. The people down here were also back and each stared at her in shock and concern.

"You alright, missy?" the old man asked. "You were walking straight out there. You woulda been killed."

Tess, shaken, nodded to the man. "Thank you, I'm sorry. I'm so sorry."

"Don't be sorry to me," the old man replied as he turned away. "Watch out next time."

After he had left and she had regained her faculties, the nausea subsided. Tess walked over to the stairwell and went up to the city street level.

She stepped into the fresh air and bright sunlight in a daze. Ahead, a newspaper machine displayed that day's paper.

"Cop Killed," the paper boldly stated, with a subheading saying: "Suspected Pentagram Link." Below, a picture of Carmen in her police blues and cap, smiling outward.

Stunned and with a gasp, Tess raised her hand to her mouth as she stepped back. Resting against the wall next to the stairwell entrance.

In through her nose and out through her mouth, she forced herself to steady her breathing, unable to look away from Carmen's picture. She was the one she had seen in her last vision. The vision she had called Detective Logan about.

———

Commander James Perkins was in his glass-paneled office, sitting in a high-back chair behind a large desk. He stared up at the two men standing in front of him. He could not hide the stress he was under.

"We've got major damage control to do here," Lieutenant Grimes said as he shook his head, causing his double chin to wobble like a turkey's. "You know how this city'll freak out if they think this pentagram thing still ain't over?"

Standing beside him, Logan was silent.

Grimes continued. "We've got to play down the cult angle of all this. Say it's probably a copycat, another crazy out there wanting some media attention, or tell them we think it could be someone who knew her. Could be her boyfriend? Anything."

"That would be a huge problem," Logan said. "We got a witness placing him at home the entire night. Carmen's mother."

Frustrated, Perkins rolled his eyes. "I don't want to hear problems, Russ." His voice was measured and stern. "Shit flows downward, you know? And the

Chief has been shitting over me all morning and the mayor on him. We guaranteed this city that Channing was *the* guy. The *only* guy. We made a mighty hoo-hah about that. Short of putting on a goddamn parade."

Logan opened his mouth. "I—"

"We told everyone it was only him," Perkins continued. "No associates. No cult. No more danger. One asshole working alone." He glared at Logan. "Not to mention us going out on a huge limb to accommodate the death penalty transfer to Nevada. We got a significant amount of egg on our faces right about now."

"With all due respect," Grimes added as he cast an accusatory glance at Logan. "We haven't just got egg on our faces. We got the whole damn omelet. Channing had us fooled. No wonder he took the fall and wanted to be put down. He was protecting the others. And you missed that whole thing, Logan."

The door to the office opened as Franklin stuck his head in.

"Sorry to butt in, sir, but we may have a witness," he said before turning to Logan. "She wants to talk to you, only you. Won't talk to anyone else. Could be a crank, but she said it was urgent."

As Logan went to walk out, Grimes grunted with disapproval. "Not so fast, Logan." He then turned to Perkins. "Commander, this should not be his case. We've already seen the price of moving too quick on this thing. This all went to shit because it was done at a speed Logan was responsible for. We need a proper senior detective on this who's not colored by the past. We need fresh blood here."

Logan stared at Grimes as he contained his anger. "We already had fresh blood. Carmen."

"Lieutenant, your objection is noted," Perkins cut in. "Russ, it's your ball. Run with it." He waved dismissively at them. "Now, both of you, get the hell out of my office."

EMERGENCE

The police interrogation room was one of the smallest in the precinct. Intentionally too small for a few people to be comfortable in. Painted gray with narrow walls and high ceilings, it was overly lit, with exposed bulbs shining down. This room was designed to make the person being questioned here want to leave as fast as they could to confess and get the ordeal over with.

In the middle of the room, a cold metal table sat, alongside metal chairs on either side, all of which were bolted to the floor. A small black tape recorder sat on one side of the table, waiting to record all confessions.

Tess sat on one of these chairs, looking uncomfortably at the imposing decor.

On the wall opposite her was a large one-way mirror that reflected the small room. On the other side of this, in an observation room, Logan and Franklin peered in. Sizing Tess up covertly.

"Doesn't look like a nut," Franklin shrugged. "Nice threads. Good-looking. Looks harmless enough. Maybe she's on the level."

"Always remember Beatrice Abernathy," Logan muttered.

"Who?"

"First big case I was put on in homicide," Logan stated as his eyes stayed fixed on Tess. "Eighty-six years old. Frail. Tiny, *tiny* woman. I'm talking less than four feet here. Sweetest old lady you've ever met. You only had to meet her once, and you'd want her to be your grandma."

"And what about her?"

"Said she witnessed the guy that raped and killed a coed who lived in the rental opposite. Said she saw the whole attack while she was sitting down watching Jeopardy. She was our star witness. Her memory was exact. Sharp as a tack. We had sketch artists mockup the person she saw, who she said she could see as clear as day. She may have been eighty-six, but her eyesight was better than mine." Logan paused as he thought. "We got lucky, though. Turned out there was a CCTV camera hidden in a store below the apartment where she lived. No one knew it was there. The camera looked straight out the shop window and had a clear shot of the coed's apartment. Saw and recorded the whole thing." He turned to Franklin with a stony expression. "Beatrice Abernathy didn't like the coed. We got her on camera, doing the whole thing."

"Wait, you said raped and killed?"

"Beatrice Abernathy was, in fact, Arthur Abernathy. We found Beatrice, his wife of fifty years, murdered, and in the bed where he slept, rotting away. He dressed up as her and lived like her for over a decade. Kept her body. Fooled everyone. Everyone saw a sweet old lady. Didn't see the truth 'cause of how she looked and acted."

"What the hell, man?" Franklin said in shock. "Why the hell did you tell me that?"

"Gotta remind yourself. No one's harmless. No one," Logan replied, walking out of the room. "Remember it. Just cos they look one way, don't mean shit."

In the interrogation room, Logan sat opposite Tess, ignoring the strange look she gave him, an unfocused, dreamlike gaze. With a pocket notebook out in front of him, he held a Biro and wrote the date and time on the first available blank page.

"My name is Detective Logan... Miss?"

"Seaton," Tess replied meekly. "Tess Seaton. Teresa. I didn't know what to do. I don't *want* to come here. But calling didn't work before."

"My partner tells me you know who we're looking for?" He glanced up from his notepad and noticed that her glassy look had changed to a more focused one as if she had woken from a dream. Her eyes were penetrating and almost unnerving as they met his. "Why don't you tell me what you know about the officer's death?"

Tess took a sharp breath in and stood from the table.

"Ms. Seaton?"

She stepped back and closed her eyes tightly, holding her palms out as her breathing increased.

"Are you okay?"

"I'll be fine," Tess replied.

"You seem frightened, Ms. Seaton." As Logan spoke, he glanced over his shoulder back into the mirror, where Franklin looked in and shrugged.

"Frightened?" she muttered with a nervous laugh. "You could say that." She then wiped her face with her hands.

"Whatever you're frightened of—"

"Let me guess, the police will protect me?"

With a surprised reaction, Logan nodded. "Exactly."

Her nervous laughter increased.

"Ms. Seaton?"

"You have zero idea. You don't have the first who killed her."

Logan sat back from his notebook and looked up at her blankly.

Guarded. Could she have killed Carm?

"Why don't you tell me?"

Looking confused at the question, she stepped closer to the table. "*Him.*"

"Who is him?"

"Channing!" she almost shouted. "Patrick Channing. The Pentagram Killer."

Though he could not hear Franklin, he knew his partner was in the observation room right at that very moment, laughing uncontrollably, holding his mouth, trying to stop the noise from bleeding through the mirror.

"I don't have time for these games." Logan closed his notebook and was about to stand. "You're wasting police time."

"Games?" she shouted. "You talk about games? I saw you and every other cop celebrating his death like it was a party. What is it you said in that report? 'Bye-bye, Patrick, don't let the door hit you on the way out'?"

He couldn't help but smirk at that. He was very proud of that response.

"Well, it's not so funny, 'cause he's back!" She leaned over the table as her voice trembled again. "You executed his body, but his spirit was set free."

Logan put his closed notebook and pen in his hand and stood. "Spirit... sure."

"That's right, his spirit! So, you bet I'm frightened. I'm *terrified*!"

"Well, thank you for coming in, Ms. Seaton," he said as he reached for the door handle.

"Don't patronize me," she said, agitated. "I'm not some crackpot off the street looking for your attention. I'm a professional psychic."

Logan did not even attempt to hide his amusement.

"And I do work for several prominent people. I helped the St. Louis Police Department find a missing child and—"

"This isn't a missing child."

"You don't think I know that? It's murder. Plain and simple. Except there's nothing simple about this. There will be many, many more, you know?"

At this last phrase, Logan paused, with the door open in front of him.

"You're not dealing with a man anymore. He has become a force. Someone as dedicated to the darkness as Channing was, feeds his power. That's why his execution did nothing but make him stronger!"

"Certainly an interesting theory you have."

Tess spoke with urgency as she stepped closer to him. "You don't understand. *You're* the one he wants. He is going to do everything in his infernal power to make you suffer and then he will kill you, too."

"Is that a threat?"

"From him? Yes. You've never had to deal with anything like this before!"

Logan nodded politely. "Well, thank you for your concern. I promise we will do our very best."

As he walked out, Tess sighed. "You've already broken one promise to me, Detective."

Logan stopped and looked back at her.

"You promised me no death penalty after I told you where he was. *You lied.*"

Stunned, Logan stepped back into the room and closed the door behind him. "*You?*" He looked at her curiously. "I should thank you, but it's obvious you knew Channing. How well did you know him? Were you a member of his cult?"

"Know? I didn't *know* him."

"But you knew where he was going to kill someone?"

"I try to stay away from murders, but when I saw the picture of the poor little girl he killed, I connected with him. As I said quite clearly, I'm a psychic."

"You connected? Where?"

"Psychically. Not physically. I opened myself up to his presence. And I never felt such rage." She shivered, remembering the feeling. "Such... evil."

"And I suppose you used these magic powers to get my unlisted phone number?"

His voice was calm, but he was annoyed and confused.

Tess smiled. "I'm sure you'd like to think that, but, no. I have a friend who works for the phone company. It's not rocket science."

Logan was not looking amused.

"Look, I didn't want publicity. I don't want thanks. I don't want money. I only want to help. My name splashed over the papers like I was some kind of freak is not something I want. I don't want people to look at me like you're looking at me. I proved my ability to you. I helped you. I told you not to allow an execution. But *you lied*. You broke your promise." She sounded more hurt than angry. "So, now he's after you, and also after me for finding him... I felt his presence, and he felt mine. It's not revenge. It's his game."

A sudden knock came from the door.

Franklin walked in and whispered into Logan's ear with urgency. "Cut her loose. We *got* him," he said with a smile.

Logan, wide-eyed, turned to Tess. "I gotta go."

"What's going on?" Tess complained.

"You should be able to psychically answer that."

"This is *important!*" She then rummaged in her bag, brought out a business card, and handed it to him. "Please call me. There is so much more I must tell you."

Tess was then left alone in the interrogation room, staring at her reflection.

"What the fuck's going on?" Logan asked Franklin. "They got him?"

"Yeah, just brought him in. He's down in holding."

Getting to the top of a stairwell, Logan pointed at the interrogation room. "Get Maz to stick to her, okay? Don't let her out of his sight."

"Shouldn't we tell him about the guy?"

"Not yet." Logan shook his head. "Otherwise, that guy won't even make it to court. Keep it on the down low for now."

In the lower level of the station, Commander

Perkins stood outside the barred holding cells, looking into one. Logan stood by his side.

In the cell, a bedraggled, skeletal man, a junkie in his late twenties, dressed in dirty trousers and a T-shirt was covered head to foot in dried bloodstains. His blotchy pale skin was heavily speckled with dry spatter. He sat rigidly on the cell bench, staring off into nothingness. His mouth hung slackly open as a large police officer stood over him.

"You killed her, didn't you?" the officer screamed into the man's face. "Admit it, asshole!"

But the man didn't flinch. He didn't even blink.

"He's been like that since they found him in an alley near Elysian," Perkins said as he shook his head ruefully. "Even had the damned murder weapon still in his hand. More or less a slam dunk, don't you think?"

Logan stared at the man, examining him. "We know who he is?"

"No ID," Perkins replied. "A junkie with track marks all over his body." He took a breath in. "Some people idolize the president. Some the pope. This scumbag chose a serial killer."

Inside the cell, the large officer stepped back from the man and turned to the commander through the bars. "I dunno what this guy's vegged on. But he's ready for the salad bar."

Taking a lighter from his pocket, Logan stepped into the cell without a word. Staring intently into the man's unblinking eyes as he got closer.

Crouching, Logan flicked his light open and then ignited the flame.

"What are you doing?" Perkins asked.

Without answering, Logan held the lighter close to the man's eyes. Looking for any reaction. To pull the man out of this possible vegetative act. But the orange flame moved unnervingly close to the man's eyes, less than an inch away, as he wafted the flame across from the left to right one. The heat didn't even cause the man to blink.

"He's not acting this, whatever it is," Logan said as he put the lighter back in his pocket. Standing straight, he took a step out of the cell.

"See you around, buddy boy," came the sickly familiar voice from behind him.

The sadistic voice of Channing.

Spinning back, Logan could see that the man on the bench had not moved. His mouth still hung half open, he had not spoken a word.

Logan then turned to the officer next to him. "What did you say?"

"What?" the officer replied, puzzled. He glanced at the commander, then back to Logan. "I didn't say a thing."

But that voice. Logan heard that voice. He *heard* it.

Perkins looked at him with concern.

In the bathroom, Logan stared at himself in the mirror. As well as the huge mental strain he was under, his wound was shooting pain through his nerves once more.

Taking the newly refilled bottle from his pocket, he took two pills, one more than he should have, then glugged some water from the tap.

The doctor's words replayed in his mind. *You say you lost your medication. But I can see, from looking at your pupils, that you've taken over your prescribed dose. So, to be on the safe side, I will give you two days' worth. Then at the end of that, you can come collect another two days and so on. Do you understand?*

He knew he shouldn't have taken both, but he needed the pain to go away. He would not take any more tonight and would deal with the pain when he got home. For now, he needed to focus without the agonizing distraction.

From the bathroom, he exited onto the main corridor, where Franklin stood and waited for him.

"You okay, man? Commander told what happened down there."

"You saw that guy, right?"

"Yeah, why?"

"I dunno." Logan shrugged. "He didn't look like he could kill anyone, did he? He can't even stand on his own two feet."

"He's out of it, for sure. Could be in shock, maybe?"

"And our little psychic friend happened to walk in at the same time as he got caught?" Logan added in

annoyance. "Bullshit. It's all a setup. Too coincidental."
He pulled the business card from his pocket.

Tess Seaton
Business and Personal Consultations
2642 Rockledge Road
By Appointment only

"Radio Maz, see where he is," Logan said as he
read the card. "We should do an uninvited house call if
she is out."

East of Runyon Canyon, a sleek mid-century style
house sat on the crest of the Hollywood Hills. The
afternoon sun in the distance colored the sky like fire
above its roof. The plants that grew on the hills around,
once verdant and green, were turning pale in the
unforgiving heat.

Logan and Franklin got out of their sedan, then
walked up the path to the front door of 2642
Rockledge.

Ringing the bell, they both waited for an answer.
But no one came. They did not expect anyone to, not
after Mazza had told them he was busy following Tess
around the shops.

Logan blinked heavily as he stared through the
glass in the door. The pain in his side had dulled, and
his head felt like it was filled with cotton candy. He
tried to remain focused, hiding any possible debilita-
tion from his partner.

"Guess it's just her in here?" Franklin said as he pressed the bell again.

Still no response.

"Should we call in for a warrant?"

The lock to 2642 Rockledge clicked as the front door opened inward to the empty house.

"We'll tell the judge we had a psychic hunch." Logan smiled as he slipped the lockpick back into its leather pouch, then into his pocket.

They both walked into the hallway, closed the door behind them, then crossed into a tastefully furnished living room. Abstract mandala art decorated the wide walls in large gold-colored frames. All of them led to a wide set of full-length windows that opened into a breathtaking panoramic city view.

"Looks like the psychic biz pays pretty damn well," Franklin said, impressed. "I definitely chose the wrong profession. I should have become the Great Franklini!" He laughed at his own joke.

Through the dining room and into Tess's office, they had discovered more psychic tchotchkes. The kind you would buy in a cheap market. Crystals, tarot decks, and a wealth of other esoteric paraphernalia littered the shelves, but there was nothing of immediate interest.

Logan stopped at a desk at the far end of the room. A computer sat on it, its monitor still switched on. An astrological chart filled the screen's desktop background.

"*Horoscopes, Past Lives, Wall Street, Sports,*" Logan read aloud the names of some folders on the screen. He shook his head in amazement. "That's what she's into, I guess."

Franklin chuckled. "She sounds like a mix of a psychic Jimmy the Greek, the Wall Street Journal and Shirley MacLaine." He scanned a large bookshelf and started looking at some titles. "Listen to these: *Esoteric Astrology, Witchcraft, and Demonology, Externalization of the Angelic Hierarchy.*"

"Nice normal reading," Logan replied as he peered into the desk's top drawer.

Nothing out of the ordinary. Only a collection of used stationery and some blank paper.

Then he opened the bottom drawer. A manilla folder sat at the top of a pile of others. On the front was written in bold ink, *Pentagram.*

Taking it out and opening it, he flicked through the large collection of newspaper clippings piled inside. News reports of the murders, the capture, the trial, as well as the execution. All collected and collated. At the bottom of this pile was a printout, at the top of which said *Russell Logan.*

"Look at this," he said, showing Franklin, who was browsing the shelves behind them. "It's got my name on it."

Glancing over at the symbols on the page, Franklin smirked. "That's your horoscope."

"What?" Logan took a closer look and read aloud

from the paper. "This Taurus is basically good-hearted—"

"Basically?" Franklin scoffed. "Sounds like an underhanded compliment to me."

"But like all his mature male bovine brethren, can be a somewhat of a stubborn bull." Logan smirked. "Now, *this* is bull."

"Look out, she's probably got a voodoo love doll of you around here, too."

———

Less than a mile away, Tess was at the counter of Antonio's, a small, high-end grocery store, whose shelves were lined with imported cheeses and countless gourmet ingredients. Antonio "Tony" Bianchi Jr., son of the store's namesake, was behind the register, ringing up Tess's purchases. He was a small bald man in his sixties and seemed perpetually happy, always with a smile for his customers.

"I put in that cheese you like as well." Antonio beamed. "No charge."

"Thanks, Tony, you didn't have to do that."

"Ah, you did me a solid on the Lakers-Suns game on Monday. Lakers by seven, just like you said." He then picked up a bag of fruit from the counter behind him and put it in her bag. "Have this, too. Least I can do."

Tess nodded, grateful.

"One thing I wanted to ask you, though, if you got time," Tony added, looking anxious. "You got any feelings about tonight's game against the Pacers?"

"Pacers by one, I think." Tess shrugged. "Feels like overtime."

"Aw shit, I bet on L.A."

From the other end of the store, behind a rotating display, Mazza watched them surreptitiously as Tess paid for her groceries. She then bid farewell to Tony and left the shop, oblivious to his presence.

Waiting for a couple of beats, he put down the packet of pasta he had pretended to read, then left after her.

Stepping onto the sidewalk, he turned left, expecting to see Tess walking toward her car, but there was no one. Not a soul around. Confused, he turned the other way, nothing.

"Looking for something?" Tess said as she stood in the next store's doorway. She walked over toward Mazza with an annoyed expression. "You've been following me for the last two blocks. *Why?*"

"You're crazy, lady," Mazza said as he stepped back. "I'm just out looking for some pasta."

"Don't lie to me, you creep," she added, pointing at him.

Not knowing how to handle this, having never been caught while tailing a suspect before, Mazza kept silent.

"Leave me alone before I call the cops!" She then stormed off in the direction of her car.

Mazza tutted. "Some psychic," he muttered as he watched her walk away.

He found it infinitely funny that she could not divine that he was a cop.

Now standing in the kitchen, Logan looked down at the blinking 3 on the answering machine display and hit the playback button.

Franklin was upstairs in one of the bedrooms, searching through piles of paperwork he had found in a collection of old filing boxes.

The answer phone beeped before playing the message. "My name's Andrea Gregg. You were recommended by my cousin, Vera Rosenberg. She says you're the most accurate psychic she's ever seen. I'd like to set up a reading if possible? You can reach me on 555-0511. Speak soon."

Logan listened to the messages as he opened the kitchen cabinets, checking each one.

The answer phone beeped again with the next message. "It's Paul." The man's voice sounded morose and distracted. "Look... I don't know how to say this, but I gotta cancel Friday. It's all a bit too weird for me." He paused. "You knowing what I'm thinking before I do? I... I just can't. And I know I should have told you to your face, but I guess I'm too chickenshit. You obviously know that, though. Bye, Tess."

Another beep. Message 3.

Instead of someone talking, the speaker painfully rang out with a collision of different static frequencies, all crackling along together. Before Logan had a chance to turn it off, a voice split through the static. Distorted. Faint. Twisted.

"Looks like the score's 16-1, buddy boy!" the voice of Channing said through all the noise. "But I guess not even 1, eh?"

Logan rushed over in a panic to the machine, listening intently to the voice.

Did I hear that? he thought as his mind raced. *No. It's impossible. It must be the meds.*

"One by one, all you dear little piggies will become mine." The voice was almost lost in the white noise. "Then, after they've all been taken, I'll take you, too."

Logan strained to hear as a cold sweat broke out on his forehead.

"How about a romantic rendezvous, you and me?"

The voice was faint, but it was unmistakable who it was.

Logan shook his head. Trying to focus, as the words sounded out, he felt his vision blurring slightly. He steadied himself on the counter.

"A little drive around Olvera Street? Buenos días, buddy boy."

"Franklin!" Logan called out in a panic.

Hearing his name, Franklin dropped the papers down into the box at his feet and ran to the ground floor.

Getting off the bottom step, he came to a skidding halt as the front door opened.

Seeing both men in her house, Tess could only stare in shock, almost dropping her grocery bag. But this shock was quickly replaced with anger.

"I don't believe you," Tess screamed at them as she walked into the kitchen, staring at Logan. "You broke in and have been, what, going through my things? Was that guy following me also a cop?"

Logan, regaining his composure, turned to see Franklin enter the room, looking at Tess with an apologetic look, as if his mother had caught him with his hand in the cookie jar. He spoke with a weak smile.

"Miss, we are—"

"Listen to this," Logan said as he rewound the answering machine tape.

"Those are private messages," Tess protested. "You can't do that!"

Logan glared at her. "After what I heard, trust me, I *can* do this."

Hitting the play button, a message repeated. "And I know I should have told you to your face, but I guess I'm too chickenshit. Bye, Tess."

Mortified, Tess slammed her grocery bag on the counter next to the answering machine and stared daggers at Logan. "How dare you!"

She sounded as if on the verge of screaming and crying at once when she reached forward to turn off the machine, but Logan batted her hand away.

"It's the next one," he said to Franklin before turning back to Tess, lifting his finger to her. "You stay there and shut up."

The answer machine beeped, as Logan dreaded hearing the voice again but *needed* to hear it.

A soft grinding static played out of the small speaker as Logan stared at it expectantly.

Nothing else played. Only static.

"What was it?" Franklin asked, walking up to the counter.

Logan's thoughts raced. He tried to piece this together.

"He was *there*," he mumbled as he tried to focus. "There were three messages. *He* was there..."

"It only says two, Russ," Franklin replied, noticing the display. "Maybe you erased it?"

"I didn't erase shit," Logan said as he stared at the number 2 on the display, as it blinked almost mockingly at him. "It was *him*!"

"Who?" Franklin asked.

"Him!" Logan was frantic. "Channing. *Patrick fucking Channing was on there!*"

Tess watched Logan as she looked down at the answering machine.

"He's dead," Franklin said with concern. "You know he's dead."

Catching his look, Logan thinly smiled as he corrected his outburst. "I mean someone trying to *be* him. Imitating his voice. Not actually him."

"And what if it *was* Channing?" Tess added.

Logan shot her a sudden glance. "I don't want to hear any more of that horseshit. No more goblins or goddamn tooth fairies. You're gonna tell me about your friends."

"I don't understand," Tess replied. "I proved to you what I can do."

"Look, this yuppie psychic routine doesn't cut it. Okay? So, what is it?"

Logan's words were icy and spoken with disdain.

"What?" she said, looking to Franklin for some help.

"You're in the same cult as Channing was?" Logan continued. "Were you fucking him?"

"Hey, Russ, let's sit down and—"

"You let us know where he was so you could get rid of him? You wanted to become the high mucky-muck now or something?"

She tried to say, "I think—"

"Tell me, is it *your* feet the disciples now kiss when they drink the virgin's blood? Or whatever it is you get off on?"

Taking offense, Tess shook her head. "I guess that's all your mind can handle, isn't it? That it's a cult? That I am obviously evil."

"Well, what else do you think it could be?"

Franklin stood by, not knowing what to do. Seeing Logan slightly losing a grip on his position.

115

"You're up against something that is beyond your wildest nightmares."

Tess spoke calmly.

Logan rubbed his eyes. "I bet it was your idea to leave that junkie zombie in the alley, trying to set him up for killing Carmen."

"You think I'm the killer?"

Logan walked around the counter and in front of her, staring at her. "Aren't you surprised? Spoils your little story, doesn't it?"

He was trying to keep his cool but failing.

Tess shook her head in disappointment. "Detective Logan. What you found was probably a poor soul that *he* took, used, then spat out. This kind of evil—"

With a burst of frustration, Logan grabbed Tess by the arms, his eyes feverish. "Stop fucking with me. There's a woman dead. *My friend* is dead! And you had something to do with it."

"You're hurting me," Tess cried out, trying to shake him off. "Let go!"

"Russ!" Franklin shouted as he rushed over and pushed his way between them. "Other room. *Now!*"

Dragging Logan out of the kitchen, Franklin spoke in a hushed, serious tone. "I don't care that you are more senior than me. I don't care that you are older than me."

"What the—"

"Shut the hell up!" Franklin shouted his whispers. "What in the living fuck is wrong with you? I get you are upset about Carm. I get that you're still injured. But you *can't* speak to a suspect like that."

Logan went to speak, but Franklin raised his palm, silencing him.

His words then slowed. "What you are doing here, *if she is the criminal*, will get the case thrown out of court. You get that, right?"

At that moment, Logan's anger dropped. He did get it.

Franklin continued. "Now I've seen enough junkies in my time to know when someone is buzzin' on luckies. So, whatever bullshit wave you're ridin' on now, if you are gonna come to the job, you cut that shit out. If not, if you are in too much pain and must take 'em, stay the fuck at home."

With a small nod, Logan tried to concentrate. Trying to regain some composure. He knew he was less in control than normal, but every bone in his body told him that something bad was happening.

"Now, go play nice," Franklin added. "We can't have this shit biting us in the ass."

"She's *part* of it," Logan said.

"Okay, fine. Then, let's take her downtown sort it out by the book."

As Logan walked back into the kitchen, he smiled at Tess. Using all his will to hide his suspicions.

"Ms. Seaton," he said, followed by Franklin. "We need to take you to the station."

Tess stared at him, still in shock from his outburst.

"You're okay, though?" Franklin asked, putting one hand on her shoulder. "Can I get you a glass of water before we go?"

With his touch, Tess felt a jolt of electricity as her gaze fell from his eyes. Her blood ran cold.

Around Franklin's neck, on a black chain, Tess saw a pentagram hanging, dripping with blood that seeped into the open collar of his shirt.

With a gasp, she blinked forcefully. Pushing the vision away. She then looked back; the bloody pentagram shifting to what actually hung around his neck, a silver Saint Christopher.

"You're in danger," she couldn't help saying as she stared at him.

Franklin felt a chill as he saw the sincerity in her eyes.

"That's it," Logan said, losing his cool again. "Save it for your paying customers." He looked at Franklin. "We gotta take her somewhere else before the station, okay?"

"Where?" she demanded.

"A romantic drive around, that's all. Isn't that what your friend said?"

———

Under the blistering late afternoon sun, the police sedan had pulled up on the street beside the park that led onto Olvera Street. Droves of people were dressed in gaily colored costumes, celebrating a summer fiesta as families and tourists wandered around. Even a few horse and cart rides were for hire, riding around the encircling paths of the El Pueblo de Los Angeles monument in the middle of the park. Vibrant banners of papel picado hung from the trees, fluttering lazily on the breeze. Their vivid blues, reds, and yellows added to the carnival feel.

The air was thick. Heavy with the scents of grilled meats and caramelized sugar that wafted over from the food vendors on Olvera Street. A street lined with a length of adobe clay buildings, with dozens of brightly colored market stalls and shops running down its pedestrianized cobblestones.

At the sedan, Logan opened the back door, allowing Tess to step out. As she did and saw the throng of people in the park, she blanched, terrified suddenly.

"We can't stay here," she said in a panic.

"Why, we too close?" Logan asked, not paying attention. He held her by the arm and led her across the path onto the grass. "Keep your eyes peeled," he called back to Franklin.

Franklin, though, was looking around, worried. "I don't like this, Russ. Tell me why the hell we're here again?"

"No, *please...*" Tess persisted. "He's near." She tried her best to pull out of Logan's grip, but it was useless. "Channing's here. We *must* go. Please."

"The voice on the machine said Olvera Street, right?" Logan said, ignoring Tess's protestations. "So, here we are."

"What voice?" Franklin asked as he followed them.

"You're right. I must have erased it by accident, but I *did* hear it. I promise you that."

Tess turned to Franklin in desperation. "Please, I told you where he was before, didn't I? I was right, wasn't I? Well, I'm telling you now, he is *here*. Please. We have to go. *You* have to go."

Logan, annoyed, noticed Franklin's increasing concern. "Come on, this is stupid. Channing is *dead*."

"I dunno about you, Russ," Franklin spoke with a tremble. "But this shit's spooky. What if she's on the level? You ever considered that?"

"Gimme a break," Logan exhaled in a hushed voice.

"What? You never experienced shit that you can't explain before?" Franklin absentmindedly reached up and held his Saint Christopher medallion as he spoke. "There's this bruja in my neighborhood. She sells love potions. I thought they were trash at first, till she got one of my friends. He hated this girl before. Then boom, madly in love. Real unnatural shit."

"Come on," Logan complained. "There're dozens of freaks that promise that shit on Hollywood Boulevard. We've busted enough of them in our time."

"I'm serious," Franklin said uneasily, nodding to Tess. "You see the way she looked at me? I can tell how much she believes it. That's enough for me to know some shit is happening. You know I love my God, but I also know there's a lot more shit out there besides Him."

The throng of people in the park seemed to grow as their noise became louder and more celebratory by the second.

"Look, if *she* doesn't want to be here, then it means, as sure as shit, this is the place *I* want to be." He stared at Franklin, at his worry, and tried to speak assuredly. "These are the freaks who killed Carm. We owe it to her to at least check this out. We will go straight to the station after. If I'm wrong, I'll take some leave, okay?"

Stepping across the grass to Olvera Street, through groups of people, the colors from the costumes seemed to glow in Logan's vision. He shook it off.

Please, not now, he thought.

Tess's eyes widened in fear as she saw a horse and cart speeding up the path behind them. People moved out of its way with shocked yells. With its old Spanish-style aesthetic and long colorful tassels hanging off, the roof to the cart had been pulled up, casting a thick shadow over the driver inside. The horse's hooves clip-clopped louder and louder on the concrete as it galloped faster.

"He's here!" Tess screamed.

As Logan turned, time seemed to slow down but not as much that he could change the course of what played out. He watched helplessly as Franklin stood there, unaware of what was approaching violently behind him.

"No!" Logan shouted.

Franklin had only an instant to turn before the horse slammed into him, sending him sprawling onto the hard concrete path below. The air shot from his lungs in a strangled gasp, and he tried to scramble away, but there was no time.

With a guttural snort, the horse reared up, its massive, powerful hooves pawing the air before it crashed down with force. Franklin screamed a high, helpless wail, which was then cut short by the sickening thud. He uselessly threw his arms up to protect himself.

The horse let out an enraged whinny as it reared up again, looming over Franklin as its hooves shot down again, cracking into his ribs. Another one of the hooves then slammed down onto Franklin's skull, cracking it inward and splitting his eye socket in half. His brain was exposed through the cracked open bone.

A spray of blood arced up through his broken skin as Franklin's gargled screams were eclipsed by other screams around him, then the boom of a gunshot from Logan's revolver.

Pointing his weapon into the air, Logan fired again and again, frightening the horse into bolting across the path with the carriage in tow.

People around stared in shock and horror, unable to fathom what they were witnessing.

Logan, with Tess on his heels, raced to the bloodied Franklin, who was lying in a heap, blood spurting from his face as he tried to gasp for breath. One eye was wide and terrified, as the other was destroyed, along with half of his skull under the horse's weight.

He stared at Logan, terrified. "Russ," he managed to gargle in agony.

"It's okay, buddy," Logan said, trying to keep calm. He then looked up and screamed at the surrounding people. "*Someone call an ambulance.*"

"Russ," Franklin repeated. "I saw him." His words were suffocated and drowning in his fluids. "It was *him*! Driving that cart. I saw him."

Before he could say another word, more blood seeped from his mouth as he began to choke. Then, within a few seconds, as the red liquid pulsed out from his face as well as flooding his lungs, he was gone in a second.

"Ambulance'll be here in a couple of minutes," a cabbie shouted from nearby, not realizing the futility of what he had said.

Looking up, fighting his anger and grief, Logan spotted the carriage speeding away in the distance. He then glanced at Franklin.

Dead and crushed.

He had to catch the man who did this.

The sedan pealed down the sidewalk, sending people scattering around, as the cars on the road sat bumper to bumper in traffic.

Tess, handcuffed to the passenger side door, looked terrified as Logan furiously drove at full speed. He kept his eyes on the cart and horse up ahead. It snaked through the bottleneck as it cut off the main road and onto a side street.

"Son of a bitch!" Logan growled.

"You heard him," Tess shouted. "He saw *him*. He *saw* Channing!"

Logan spun the wheel and plowed off the sidewalk, swerved past honking cars, and across the road's divider. As he turned the sedan down the side street, he saw the cart up ahead stopped in front of an alley. The horse stood there patiently.

Pulling up, Logan grabbed his gun, then jumped out of the car, a look of determination, upset, and fury mixed all over his face.

"You're only doing what he wants you to do!" Tess screamed.

Ignoring her, Logan raced over to the cart and peered inside, his gun aimed ahead.

There was nothing. The cart was empty.

Echoing footsteps from the alley ahead then dragged his attention. Whirling around, Logan spotted a figure running.

Without a thought, he gave chase, leaving Tess handcuffed in the sedan.

He could not hear her shout helplessly.

"He's going to kill you!"

REVELATION

Logan sprinted down the alley, each heavy step jarring his injury, shooting a searing pain up his side. He didn't have to look, he *knew* he was bleeding through his bandage, having probably split the stitches yet again.

Ahead, the figure pulled open a grimy door to a dilapidated tenement building and slipped inside, disappearing from view.

Gritting his teeth, Logan forced himself to keep going, following the figure.

He *had* to catch him.

That was all he could think. If he did not, the haunting image of Franklin would be tearing him apart with grief.

The tenement's interior was worse than Logan had expected. Peeling paint covered the walls in wide, curling strips, as garbage and broken furniture littered the narrow hallway. A thick stench of sickness and human waste clung to the air, almost overpowering him as the door slammed shut behind him. This was a junkie's den, for sure.

Footsteps thundered above him, echoing down the stairwell ahead. Logan braced himself and charged upstairs, ignoring the way each step felt like a fresh knife twisting in him. He took the stairs two at a time, teeth clenched to keep from crying out as the agony clawed at his nerves, up the ten stories up to the top of the tenement.

Pigeons scattered in a panic as Logan forced the door open that led onto the flat roof. He blinked as his vision blurred, his pulse loud in his ears, the pain shooting to his temples.

He then saw the figure clearer, standing at the roof's edge. He wore a mask, a plastic, twisted mockery of a face, stretched and distorted. Molded with a permanently grotesque grin. One that was too wide to be real, with lips peeled back to reveal crude, blood-colored teeth. This mask was a caricature of gleeful malevolence. Its material was almost translucent and showed only the smallest hint of the person wearing it. Pale skin and dark hair were all that stood out. Through the recesses of this mask's cut-out sockets, hollow, sunken eyes glared out at him, glinting.

Without wasting a second, Logan raised his gun as he steadied his aim. But before he could do anything, the figure turned and leaped across the narrow gap, over to the neighboring rooftop.

"Dammit," Logan muttered.

He had no time to hesitate, so he sprinted toward the edge and launched himself into the air.

He came crashing down onto the next roof, as a jolt of agony erupted within, causing him to crumple forward. He clutched his side, a strangled cry escaping him before he could force himself unsteadily onto his feet.

He staggered forward, gun drawn, aiming at the figure standing at the edge of the roof, a roof with no building opposite to jump over to. All there was, a ten-story drop straight down onto the concrete below.

"Freeze, you son of a bitch!" Logan screamed, his voice straining. He tried to focus through his torment.

Tears blurred his vision as he struggled to keep his aim on the figure.

The figure, meanwhile, balanced effortlessly on the edge of the roof as a low chuckle escaped through the mask.

Slowly, the figure raised his hands in surrender.

Reaching for his cuffs, Logan's heart sank as he remembered he'd left them in the car with Tess.

The figure tilted his head and let out another small laugh. Then, with no hesitation, they leaned back and plummeted over the side.

Logan raced to the edge, peering down in horror, expecting to witness the grisly impact of the figure's body shattering in a wet heap on the street below. Instead, he watched in shock as the figure twisted in midair and then landed gracefully on his feet like a cat. Impossibly unhurt.

The figure then peered back up to the roof, to Logan. With a mocking wave, he then took off down the street, hurriedly sprinting away.

Logan's head throbbed, the shock of what he'd witnessed, mixed with the pain in his body, threatened to overwhelm him. Without a second thought, he clambered over the edge and onto the nearby fire escape, ignoring the protest from his aching body and began an unsteady descent to the ground level.

When he finally reached the street, he looked frantically in every direction, but the figure had vanished from the scene without a trace.

Nearby, two men stood leaning against their car, who Logan could tell were in a gang, but he didn't care enough to worry.

"Where'd he go?" Logan asked as he struggled to catch his breath.

"Who?" one of the men asked.

Logan motioned to the tenement in frustrated anger. "The guy that just jumped off this fucking building! Who do you think, Babe Ruth?"

The men both laughed.

"Man, you trippin'," one said dismissively as the other leaned forward.

"What are you smokin'?" he asked Logan in a mock whisper. "'Cause we could sure use some of that strong shit right about now."

Logan could only feel a creeping doubt taking root in the back of his mind.

Two hours later, the same street was crawling with a dozen uniformed officers who searched every inch of the area: alleyways, buildings, parked cars. If it was there, they were looking into it.

Logan was sitting on the open back of an ambulance, his shirt off as he was having his bandage changed by a medic. He was lucky the stitches held, but that didn't stop the blood from coming out.

He watched forlornly at the fruitless search, as Commander Perkins stood beside him, thin-lipped.

"Tell me again, Russ," Perkins said. "Blow by blow. What happened? I can't get my head around what you are saying."

"What for? I already told you—"

"Because I really want to know how we go from what happened to Franklin to a man then jumping off a ten-story building and walking away without a scratch."

As Perkins spoke, his frustration was evident.

A wave of grief hit Logan as he recalled what happened to Franklin. His contorted body on the ground in agony, his one eye staring at him, pleading for rescue, his other a smashed paste in his caved-in eye socket.

"You left Franklin there, dead, in a public place. What were you thinking?" Perkins looked at Logan in confusion. "I get you were upset, but, Russ. Come on."

"I wanted to catch the guy," Logan replied. "Franklin was dead. I couldn't help him... I..."

A lump hitched in his throat.

The medic finished wrapping his bandage as he handed Logan his bloodstained shirt. Achingly, Logan put it back on and then buttoned it up.

Lieutenant Grimes, sweating in his uniform in the heat, strode across the road with a derisive sneer on his face. "You've caused us a whole heap of shit, Logan."

Logan only looked back helplessly.

"You know that woman whose house you broke into?" Grimes asked sarcastically. "You know, the one you abducted, then recklessly endangered the life of in a high-speed chase?"

Perkins wanted to speak up on Logan's defense, as he truly disliked Grimes. But on this point, he could not think of a single word.

Grimes looked like a cat who caught the canary. "The next time you pull a stunt like that with a member of the public, try to do it to someone who doesn't read tea leaves for the deputy mayor's wife! Her lawyer came in and got her. You want to hear about the size of the lawsuit he was talking about? Hell, let's not even mention the lawsuits we'll probably get from the public after you left a fallen officer out there." Grimes turned to Perkins, hardly concealing his anger. "Ol' supercop here didn't even check that woman's alibis before accusing her of murder. Didn't even investigate his crazy theories of murder cults or check anything about them. He went totally off the rails and opened us up to a lot of problems we didn't need right now."

Shaking his head, Grimes turned back to Logan. "You should be ashamed of yourself." He grimaced as he walked away to a squad car waiting for him.

"Look, Russ," Perkins said.

"Yeah, yeah, I know," Logan muttered. "Days ago, I was the hero of the fucking city. Today, I'm a garden variety nutcase. I get how it all looks. I really do. And I know the position I've put you in."

"Sir," a uniformed officer shouted as he hurried over, shocked. "It's Detective Mazzaro."

Those words felt like a kick in Logan's damaged gut.

———

The Los Angeles River was a trickle of browning water down the center of the aqueduct near Griffith Park. With the sun in its final throes of the day, the shadows had begun to lengthen in a dull haze. But that did not stop the unrelenting heat as the police cars drove along the river's basin, up to a large overpass.

An unholy, horrific sight, Detective Albert "Mazza."

Mazzaro was stripped naked and hanging between the beams of the overpass, strung up by his own bloody intestines. With his stomach cut open, the length of his insides had been stretched outward and pulled taut to create this terrifying tableau. One that seemed impossible to comprehend how it was even done.

Within Mazza's bloody, gaping stomach cavity, his severed head had been placed upside down. With his eyes plucked from their sockets, they hung by their stalks upon his forehead. Carved into his chest, a large pentagram had been cut.

By the time Logan, Perkins, and Grimes had arrived at the scene, uniformed officers were already standing on a cherry picker, trying to cut his body down.

"Lieutenant Grimes," Perkins said as he stared at the remains of Mazza in horror. "You will take over the investigation with immediate effect."

"Yes, sir," Grimes replied, before walking off victoriously back to his car.

Logan tried to figure out what had happened, but all he could think of was the impossible things he had witnessed, as well as the medication he was on.

"I hope I *am* nuts. I really do. Because if I'm not, then... Then I don't think any of us are gonna be much good at stopping it."

Logan didn't know what he believed and didn't know whether Tess was involved. He didn't know if she was crazy, didn't know if Franklin had seen Channing, didn't know how Mazza was strung up or the significance of his butchery. He only knew three things. One was that Channing died in the gas chamber, that someone was killing using the same MO, and that he was in no fit state to work.

Even with Grimes leading the investigation, Logan still could not bring himself to stop. Even if his badge was going to be taken away, which he thought was almost inevitable, he would carry on until he caught the killer or died trying.

But right then, he thought that the latter may be the most likely option.

As the night set in, Logan made his way back to the homicide department and sat in the darkened open-plan office on his own. A single desk lamp illuminated his workspace.

With the telephone in his hand, he stared at the photos in front of him as he spoke. Photos of Franklin at the scene of his death. Graphic and clinical, these images glared back up at him, haunting his thoughts. The half-empty bottle of scotch on his desk did nothing to quell his torment.

"Nancy?" he asked into the receiver. "Whatever I can do, okay? You gotta ask. I'm here for you and the kids twenty-four seven."

Franklin had loved his wife and children more than anything else in the world, and the thought of being the root cause of this tragedy gnawed at Logan deeply. There were so many what-ifs that plagued him as he spoke to his partner's widow. If only he hadn't been so incensed to drag them to Olvera Street. If only they had waited outside Tess's house for a warrant. If only he had called in some backup at the park. If only he had given the case to Grimes after he realized that he was in no fit state to do so.

"I'll call you tomorrow, okay? Try to get some sleep," he said before hanging up the call.

Next to the forensic photos of his partner's body was Franklin's bloodstained police badge. Staring at it, bewildered and grieving, Logan could not stop the tears that flowed as he sobbed in the quiet, dark office.

The park by Olvera Street was deserted in the early hours of the following day. The area where Franklin died had still been cordoned off with police caution tape, and the grass he had laid on was still stained red with dried blood.

Having sat there since sunrise, Logan had rued what had happened while desperately trying to figure everything out. Looking at the puzzle from all the angles that he could. When people started jogging by or walking past him to work, Logan stood and started walking.

The alcohol he'd had was a shadow that hung as a heavy reminder. Not a hangover as such, more of a thick head that reminded him that he drank far too much.

In a grief-riddled daze, it wasn't long until he found himself standing in front of a large Catholic church. With its Spanish Colonial-style facade, the front of this Abrahamic house of worship was framed by twin bell towers placed on either side, each capped with small domes and crosses. The entrance to the building was a simple, plain wooden double door.

Despite his lack of faith, he felt a pull to walk in. Memories of his youth had surfaced as he stared at the building, of Sundays when his mother would insist he enter the confessional booth to unload his sins on an expectant priest. Though he had no real interest or belief in the church's ritual, speaking to the faceless person in the confessional used to give him a strange kind of release. Like therapy but without the bill.

Maybe?

As he stepped onto the stone slabs that lined the church's floor, Logan peered around. A handful of people were there. Some prayed. Some lit candles on the votive stand. All were almost silent in reverence of where they were. When he checked his watch, it said 10:14 a.m. A lot later than he had presumed.

Have I really been out here for five hours?

Walking forward, he noticed an old woman exiting the small confessional booth at the far end of the aisle, across from the altar. Hidden in the shadows and imbued with an eerie familiarity, he stared at the confessional, unsure. But something, perhaps a lingering thread of his mother's insistence or the deep anguish that lay in his heart, pulled him to walk toward it.

The dark booth carried with it a blend of scents, worn into the wood-lined walls and well-used uphol-stered seat. Aged varnish with a faint trace of incense masked the dusty and stale odor of the fabric beneath him. As soon as he sat, he felt a quiet solemnity surround him.

Peering through the lattice partition, Logan could make out the silhouette of the priest sitting in the adjacent booth, waiting for the next parishioner to unburden themselves.

"Good morning, my child," the man said, his voice tinged with a Latino accent.

"Forgive me, Father, for I have sinned," Logan said on almost autopilot.

He would not have remembered what to say in this booth if you had asked him ten minutes prior. But right then and there, everything flooded back from his childhood.

"How long since you last confessed to the Lord, my son?"

"A long time," Logan replied, clasping his hands together. "God and I had a bit of a disagreement, so I haven't been around."

"Holy Mother, the church, accept all those who return penitent to the fold."

"Look, Father. I don't know that I'm anything close to penitent. I don't know much anymore. I thought I knew where it all stood... After my dad..." He paused as he tried to find the right words.

"Please continue, my son."

"After my dad was shot, I guess I thought that if there *was* a God, why would he take him, a guy who never did anything wrong in his life?" He shook his head. "My mom kept saying, over and over, 'It's God's will, it's God's will,' like *that* was the reason. Like that would make any of it better. I was only a kid." Taking a moment, Logan stared at the shadows at his feet, to the thin sliver of candlelight light peering through the bottom of the door.

He had not talked of his father or what had happened for years. Many years.

His mind reeled back to that night, to the policemen at their door, as the rain poured down around them. Informing his mother that her husband was dead. Her collapsing to the floor, wailing in anguish, as the nine-year-old Russell watched helplessly from the staircase. The papers reported the murder for days, as there was no reason found for it. It was a mystery that the reporters relished.

His father had his wallet still on him, with over a hundred dollars of cash inside. His expensive watch, the only thing he ever bought for himself, still ticked on his wrist. All they could tell is that he was forced to his knees and was shot at point-blank in the back of the head, execution style, in his local bar, in front of a lot of people. No one knew a thing except that two men with balaclavas walked in, walked straight up to him, forced him down, and shot him. No words were spoken. Only the action.

The biggest problem for the investigation was that his father was not a criminal. He had no enemies. He was a normal, average, everyday dad. And since, all these memories came back, having been repressed for the longest time and hit Logan hard.

For the first time since then, Logan felt that death was haunting him. Taking Franklin, Carm, and Mazza, bit by bit, whatever was happening had taken more of what he loved.

No. He shook the thoughts off. His father and the current crimes were not the same. Not about him.

"Look, Father," he said. "I've seen a lot of death. A lot of bodies. And when someone's dead, they're dead, right?"

"That was not the case for Lazarus or Jesus," the priest answered. "But please, continue."

What Tess had said and what he had seen of the catatonic junkie in the jail cell, not to mention Franklin's dying assertion, threw up so many propositions that seemed to him like asylum talk.

"I don't know. Maybe I'm going nuts. But..." He paused, making sure the question was worded correctly, as he was not entirely sure what his question was. "Can the spirits of the dead return? Like actually come back and take over bodies of people still living?"

"This is not a question I have ever heard at the confessional before but let me answer you as best as I can." The priest shuffled in his seat and turned to the lattice partition. "Scriptures have told of great saints who return to help earthly souls—"

"I don't mean a saint. I mean someone evil!"

"Oh, so you mean possession. Then, yes. Most definitely, there are many instances in the bible and throughout the history of demonology, of darkness returning from the next world on paths of hate, as the saints can use paths of light and hope."

"What do you mean by paths?"

The priest paused for a second before answering. "I'm using the terminology I was taught. No one knows how these things work. We can only speak through allegory and symbolism. Path is only a word we use, as we understand what it means: something to travel on."

"Okay, but can I ask... can they be stopped? Do you know how?"

"I do," the priest said. "But before I answer your question, I must ask you one of my own, my son. Is that okay?"

"What is it, Father?"

A low laugh then came from the priest's mouth. As he spoke, his Latino accent fell away. "How's the stomach, buddy boy?"

Logan's hair stood as he heard that familiar voice. *Channing.*

Through the lattice partition, the figure leaned in closer and the shadow on his face cleared. There was that face. The face that wore the mask with the cartoonishly sadistic grin, his eyes glimmering back at Logan through its plastic holes.

"What sound does a stuck piggy make?" the voice chuckled. "Let's see, shall we?"

Before Logan could react, the lattice partition split under the pressure of a serrated blade thrusting violently through it and toward him. The knife's edge sliced through the air, spearing deep into the opposite panel of the wooden confessional with a hollow crack, missing Logan's neck by an inch. The blade then wrenched backward, poised to strike again.

Panic and adrenaline surged in a flash as Logan rolled sideways, hitting the floor hard as he scrambled out of the booth. He gasped for air as he stumbled upright, instinctively searching for an escape, all the while hearing that dark chuckle echoing behind him.

With his gun drawn, Logan raced to the priest's door of the booth and grabbed the handle. Pulling it open, he aimed his gun, ready to fire. Fully expecting the knife to come singing out at him.

But the booth was empty.

"Ave Maria," the priest said in his fake Latino accent, coming from behind him.

Spinning on his heel, Logan whipped his aim around. His eyes were wide, and his pulse was speeding.

There, on top of the altar, the figure in the mask stood, carrying the large blade in his hand.

He turned toward Logan. "Did you know that Jesus hated cops?"

Racing toward him, Logan gripped his gun tight, and he sped past the votive stand, around the large pillars that lined the outer aisle. As the white column blocked his vision for the merest of seconds, as he got to the nave and took aim, the figure was gone.

Confused at the sudden disappearance, Logan felt a sudden cold chill.

Is any of this real?

Then a dark flash of movement in the alcove opposite caught his attention, stealing him out of his doubt.

The pain in his stomach seemed to constantly return over the past week, with every movement he made. The pain itself was not something he had gotten used to, but it was something that he had gotten used to *not* getting used to. A torment that appeared each day if he moved much. He had been expecting it since, and as expected, his injury throbbed like white-hot heat.

As he approached the alcove, he aimed his gun and readied himself.

"Freeze! LAPD!"

But, standing there, an old woman dressed in black gasped, crossing herself as she whimpered.

Lowering his gun, Logan didn't have time to explain or apologize before the petrified old woman scurried away.

Taken aback, he took a breath to steady himself, but before he could, another dark shape shot out from behind the pillar, right at him. With no time to react or fire his gun, he could only stand there as the figure took an impossible leap straight over his head.

Soaring, this figure smashed through the opposite stained-glass window to the grass outside.

Logan covered his face with his hand as glass shards splintered and smashed out in all directions.

In his wake, the man left a large, jagged hole in the glass. One that Logan followed.

Climbing through, Logan jumped out in pursuit. Across the street, he noticed the figure retreating through a vacant lot. Ignoring his pain, ignoring his panic, and most of all, his doubt.

He dashed with determination. But the figure ahead of him was fast, and the blur of black disappeared around a corner, into an adjacent backstreet, leaving only a trace of movement in its wake. Logan barely registered his surroundings as he gave chase. The world around him was spinning, as well as strangely quiet. His footsteps echoed against the cracked pavement of the lot as he ran. Sounding like a cavernous beating drum.

This backstreet stretched ahead of him as he saw the shambling figures drifting aimlessly through the thick shadows. Each of their faces was worn and hollowed, with eyes glazed over. They were like ghosts trapped in a city of ruin. These were not merely the homeless, but they were the helpless and the forgotten.

Logan could feel their stares linger as he hurriedly moved past them. These men and women, dressed in ragged clothes, glared at him like an encroaching alien in their world.

He had to stop for a second, his breath catching as his eyes darted in all directions, hoping for a glimpse, a hint of movement from the figure. But there was nothing, only the oppressive dread and searching eyes of those around him.

Farther down the street, as the throng of vagrants depleted, it gave way to dumpsters and dirt, where a bright neon hanging sign blinked. *Pico House Hotel. Rooms by the hour. No questions.*

The Pico House Hotel was a dire place. A flophouse was too kind a word for it. It was a building of tiny box rooms. Each had a small, stained mattress on a wire spring frame. A small, cracked sink sat in each of the rooms, with a rusted tap that dribbled out brown water. The people who stayed here were those who had a few more dollars than those sleeping on the streets. Those who had a fraction less filth coating their bodies. But somehow, in there, the people seemed a lot more desperate.

At the small reception desk, an old man with the longest of beards, the leatheriest of skin, and the yellowest of teeth sat in a perma-cloud of his cigarette smoke. He was the gatekeeper to this disgusting hovel of desperation and sadness.

As Logan entered, he noticed the old desk clerk, who did not even look up as he walked in. A man sat in a weathered chair at the bottom of the stairs. A man with a thousand-yard stare, who was slumped in a tattered army jacket. He looked soldered into the chair's worn fabric as if he hadn't moved for years. He stared at Logan as he walked by, and as he passed, he reached and pawed at him.

Logan, backing away from the man, kept his gun drawn as he ascended the staircase. His ears pricked as he cautiously listened for any movement ahead of him. Each step he took was slow. But no matter how hard he tried, he could not stop the wood from creaking, as if the stairs were intentionally alerting everyone of his approach.

Reaching the corridor landing, Logan crept along.

Ahead of him, the doors to each of the rooms were strangely wide open. As he approached the first one, he peered inside. The television at the far end of the dank room was blaring as a groaning man in soiled underwear lay on the browning bed opposite, a needle still stuck in his arm.

In the next room, a man and a woman were on the floor. The woman dressed in a leather miniskirt, hitched up around her waist, looked extremely uninterested as a cigarette hung from her lips. Behind her, a sweaty man thrust into her. The woman's gaze connected with Logan's, and she offered a bored yet eerily polite smile. Like a checkout cashier waiting for the shift to end.

Logan offered a thin grin in return as he walked on.

Each room he passed was as distraught and as sad as it was filthy.

Ahead of him, at the end of the hall, one door remained closed.

Room 237.

As Logan approached, he steadied himself as he stared at the numbers.

Closing his eyes for a second, he felt the pain in his side. It was getting a lot worse. It was distracting him too much when he needed his attention as much as possible. He grabbed the pill pot from his jacket and then downed two pills. Cracking them in his teeth before swallowing them dry. He hoped they might take effect faster.

As he got ready to open the door, a terrible scream sounded from down the corridor.

Logan turned, and standing at the end of the corridor was Tess Seaton. Screaming as she stared at him with wide eyes. A look of abject terror smeared over her face as she pointed. Pointed behind him.

The door to 237 opened inward to the pitch-black room inside. Before Logan could turn back to it, through the darkness, the gray head of a fire ax came swinging out.

With no time to fire, shout, or duck, the ax found its target with a violent blow.

Sliding into Logan's skull, the ax passed cleanly through bone, brain, and blood as it carved through his face. One eye burst as it went, the top of his head split to either side like an open book.

Tess screamed as she watched Logan turn to her in shock. His legs buckled as his split head glared at her before collapsing to the frayed carpet.

The masked figure stopped as it regarded the quivering corpse at his feet.

Tess's screams fell as he turned his attention to her. Though the mask he wore had a big plastic smile molded onto it, the man beneath did not have the same smile.

She turned to run, but the staircase was suddenly gone, and the corridor was a dead end. She could not figure out what was happening before she turned back and saw the figure jump up and grab a ceiling fan. Ripping it down clean off its hinges, he held it out. Its power cord trailed down from the ceiling after it.

Starting it like it was some kind of power saw, the figure then stepped closer. Holding the fast-spinning blades out to her like an approaching Cuisinart.

Tess looked around, but she couldn't escape.

The man stepped closer, while the blades of the ceiling fan spun faster and faster. The power cord behind him pulled through the ceiling's plaster as he advanced.

The whirring became deafening as it eclipsed Tess's cries for help.

Faster and faster and faster, the blades spun. As they did, the corridor spun with it.

From the floor behind him, Logan's dead eyes stared in witness.

. . .

A crystal perfume decanter shattered onto the department store floor. The liquid within burst over the fake marble tiles beneath. The garish, bright light in the store caught on the crystal shards, sending reflections of light around the department.

"Hey, watch it," a young female shop assistant shouted as Tess gripped the edge of the display counter, trying to steady herself.

Tess's eyes were rolled back in her head as she gritted her teeth.

As soon as it appeared, this vision had subsided. Tess stood there, holding the metal framed glass counter, perfume droplets having sprayed up her skirt.

She fought to regain her breath as the shop assistant worriedly walked around the counter.

"Should I call an ambulance?" the assistant asked, almost afraid to approach.

Tess blinked rapidly, clearing the vision from her eyes. Without a pause, Tess then turned and rushed out of the store, leaving the assistant standing with the wreckage of the expensive perfume decanter at her feet.

"Hey, you gotta pay for this!" she cried out after Tess, but it was too late.

Down the long, dirty street, lined with vagrants, dumpsters, and dirt, a bright neon hanging sign blinked. *Pico House Hotel. Rooms by the hour. No questions.*

Logan approached it, peering up at the sign.

He knew this place. It was a dire location he had been called to a few times over the years. Usually a suicide or someone beating up a sex worker. Either way, whenever he had been called out, it was never nice, and the building reflected that.

At the small reception desk, an old desk clerk with the longest of beards, the leatheriest of skin, and the yellowest of teeth sat in a perma-cloud of cigarette smoke. He was the gatekeeper to this disgusting kingdom of desperation and sadness.

He did not look up as Logan entered with his gun in hand.

"Hey," Logan said to the desk clerk. "I'm looking for a guy who would've just come in here. Where'd he go?"

The clerk didn't look up from the porno magazine that lay open on the desk in front of him as ash from his cigarette dropped onto the page.

Logan stood, staring at the man.

"Didn't see shit," the clerk grumbled.

Logan then hit the reception desk with his open palm, snapping the desk clerk's attention to him. Logan then opened his jacket to show the police badge on his belt.

The clerk shook his head. "Didn't see shit, *sir*." He then noticed the dark-red patch on Logan's shirt and nodded toward it. "You hurt?"

Logan looked down. His wound was bleeding *again*. And as he noticed, the pain in his body came into focus. Searing up his nerves. Grimacing, he then walked over to where the vacant veteran sat, as if soldered to the chair for years. The veteran sluggishly looked up at him.

"Hey, buddy?" Logan asked. "How about you? D'you see anyone come in here?"

Without a word, the veteran grinned a maniacal and toothless smile as he pointed up the stairs.

————

"There it is!" Tess cried out from the back seat of the taxicab. "Please hurry!"

As the yellow cab came to a quick stop outside of the Pico Hotel, Tess threw a ten-dollar bill to the driver and then bolted out of the door.

In front of the hotel entrance, homeless, destitute men crowded as they walked by in a sluggish, zombie-like daze.

"Excuse me," Tess asked as she pushed her way through the grimy clothes and stink.

Each turned to her with a cold stare as she passed. Their eyes were bright against the grime that caked their skin.

"Wanna fuck, sweetheart?" an inebriated figure slurred as he stepped out into Tess's path, grabbing his crotch.

Disgusted, she squeezed past the man and into the hotel.

Racing across the foyer, she did not even look around as she veered straight for the stairs past the toothless veteran, who watched her as she dashed by.

Ahead of Logan, at the end of the hall, one door was still closed.

Room 237.

As he approached, he looked up at the numbers on the plain door and steadied himself. Closing his eyes for a second, he realized the pain was subsiding. Maybe it was psychosomatic, as he had only just taken the pills, or maybe they were taking effect that fast. Either way, he felt some relief.

A scream came from behind him.

Logan spun, gun held out in front of him.

Standing at the end of the corridor was Tess. Screaming as she stared with wide eyes. A look of abject terror smeared over her face.

The door to 237 then opened inward to a pitch-black room. Before Logan could turn back to it, through the darkness, the gray head of a fire ax came swinging out.

With no time to fire, Logan swiveled his body and missed the sharp blade careening down from above.

As if in one single movement, the ax handle then came up and smashed into Logan's jaw, knocking him backward across the hall. His gun fell from his grasp as he slammed into the wall, collapsing to the floor.

The ax then raised again as the masked figure stepped out and loomed over Logan.

With almighty force, the ax swung, but Logan rolled out of its path again as the blade slammed into the floorboards where he sat, splintering them as it did.

Logan kicked at the embedded ax, smashing it out of the figure's hands. Then, with his elbow, he hit the figure in the kneecap.

Clambering to his feet, he readied himself for a fight.

Tess rushed down the corridor toward them "Channing! Stop!"

As the figure grasped for the ax, upon hearing that name, he stopped and turned to face her.

Logan staggered back to the wall to steady himself. His stare flitted between the two people on either side of him. Unsure of what was happening.

Tess reached into her pocket and brought out a small silver amulet. On the face of it, a pentagram was carved into the metal.

Logan stared as the figure appeared to be frozen. Entranced in the silver glare. His eyes stared unblinkingly at the pentagram. Hypnotized.

With his gun on the carpet only a couple of feet away, Logan reached between Tess and the figure.

"No! Logan!" Tess screamed urgently.

Almost immediately, the figure blinked as his view of the amulet was interrupted.

Without pause, the figure then jumped up and ripped the ceiling fan down, clean off its hinges. Its power cord trailed down after it. The figure then started the fan like it was some kind of oversized power saw. The blades spun fast. Impossibly fast in a lethal blur, as the figure stepped toward them like some kind of demonic Cuisinart.

Logan grabbed his gun and stumbled back to Tess. Dragging her back down the corridor, he turned and fired at the figure. But the bullets just hit the whirring blades, ricocheting off their rotating metal surface.

Faster and faster and faster they spun. The figures stepped closer and closer, the power cord from the fan ripping through the plaster of the ceiling behind him as he walked.

Logan pulled Tess to one side, through an open bedroom door.

In this larger room, a line of bunk beds could be made out in the dim light. Crammed together in a barracks-style, there were six beds in this room. Six filthy beds. They were the cheapest in the hotel. By the hour, beds for any purpose. *Any* purpose.

The only source of light here was a dim orange bulb that hung in the middle of the room. Its murky glow gave the room an even more seedy, dirty feel. A sickly stench of stale sweat and bodily fluids clung onto the bed's dirty sheets clumped in unmade piles on each bunk. Under a couple of these sheets, huddled dirty masses lay snoring. Drunks and junkies sleeping away the day until the nighttime would come. Until the next fix would come.

Tess and Logan had no time to consider the conditions of the room or the people within, as he turned and locked the door. Dragging Tess back toward the window, he opened it up to the fire escape on the other side.

With a thunderous slam, a tremendous force collided with the bunk room's locked door.

Then again. *Slam.*

The wood splintered with a crack under this assault.

The sleeping drunks did not stir as the door then gave way and split into three pieces before the figure broke his way through.

In the alleyway below, Logan and Tess scrambled from off the rickety metal fire escape and then raced out onto the street ahead.

Grabbing the police badge from his belt, Logan ran off the sidewalk and in front of an oncoming car. He did not know if this would even work but had to try anything he could.

Lifting his shield to the driver, he shouted, "LAPD!"

The driver of the car skidded to a halt a couple of feet in front of him. Logan looked relieved.

"What the hell are you doing?" the young man shouted out of the window as Logan raced around to his side.

"Police emergency. Move over," Logan ordered. "It's life or death."

"Look, Officer," the young man stuttered. "My

153

name's Randy Beaumont... I'm only eighteen... I'm not one of those anti-cop types, but I'm—" His face fell as he looked upward, past Logan, and to the building they had emerged from. "What the hell?"

Looking up, Tess and Logan saw what the young man saw. The masked figure stood in the open window, looking down at them from high above. The ceiling fan still in his hand.

"Move over!" Logan screamed as he yanked the driver's side door open and forcibly pushed the young man over to the passenger side. "Get in!" he cried back to Tess.

She didn't need to be told twice.

The figure in the window dropped the ceiling fan and then calmly stepped out of the window and jumped directly down toward the car.

VENGEANCE

The windshield of Randy Beaumont's car smashed outward as the masked figure landed feet first onto the car's hood. Metal beneath him crumpled as his weight landed with an almighty thud. His engine sputtered but still ran beneath.

Randy screamed in terror.

This jump did not slow the figure down, as his hand reached through the shattered windshield and grabbed Randy by the throat, strangling his scream.

Logan's foot slammed on the gas pedal with all his might, which lurched the car forward with a shriek of rubber upon asphalt. As he yanked the wheel to the right, the figure clung onto the crumpled hood and Randy's throat.

The figure then peered over to Logan, the smile on his translucent mask looking as if he was mocking their attempt to escape.

Instinctively, Logan turned the wheel back sharply to the left, sending the car hurtling across the empty street and toward a building. The figures' legs flopped off the right side of the crumpled hood.

As he drove, the opioids he had taken ramped up more effect. Warm fuzziness vibrated in his head, and the colors in his vision seemed to brighten in hue. Becoming more dreamlike. Making this horror almost seem like an amusement park ride.

Shaking it off, Logan turned the car again, aiming the car at the opposite side of the street speeding onto the adjacent sidewalk and getting the car closely parallel to the brick of the building.

The rough exterior caught the figure's dangling legs and, with what should be a fatal force, yanked him off the car. It tore his grip from the young man's throat and sent his body down between the tiny gap of the car and the exposed brickwork.

The sound of a vile crunch rang out as the figure's body was crushed against the wall and spat out behind them.

This force should have killed anyone without a single chance for survival, but Tess could not help but look back as they sped away. Through the rear window, she saw the figure stand up from the sidewalk, then brush himself down as if nothing had happened. He waved at her as they escaped.

Eleven blocks away, Logan and Tess had taken Randy Beaumont to the nearest city hospital, after he had passed out from the shock of what had happened to him. When the doctor let them know that he would be fine when he woke up, they left without another word.

Logan felt bad Randy would have a smashed car and nothing else to show for it, not even the name of the officer who commandeered his vehicle. But there was more at stake here. He made a promise to himself that if he survived this, he would make sure all was compensated with that kid. He could only imagine the looks people would give Randy when he told them the impossible things he had seen.

At a plaza, Logan and Tess had walked in silence for a few blocks. Logan was too unsure of what had happened and searched his mind for how to ask what he needed to ask her. Tess, on the other hand, was too nervous to push what she believed on this man again, especially after his reactions before.

"Miss Seaton. Uh," Logan said finally, with a wealth of trepidation around each word.

"Tess, please," she replied sheepishly.

"Tess, okay."

Another awkward pause hung between them.

"I... Look, I want to—"

"It's okay," Tess said. "You don't have to thank me."

"Do you always finish people's sentences?" Logan asked as he looked around, on edge. "Boy, I could use a drink," he mumbled before returning to the conversation. "Okay, from the beginning. What the hell's going on? And how did you know where I was? And what the hell was that coin thing you held up?"

Tess smiled thinly as she came to a stop next to a street vendor selling hot dogs.

He turned to face her as she gathered her composure.

"Please accept what I say as what *I* think. I'm not trying to force belief on an unbeliever, okay? You can take it or leave it as you want, but I think you should at least be open to the possibility. Especially after what you've seen already."

Logan nodded. Not wanting to verbally commit to anything, noticing the street vendor staring at them, listening to their conversation as he served a customer a hot dog.

Tess continued, speaking nervously. "And I'm not totally sure myself. All I know is that Patrick Channing is dead."

"We both know that."

"*But* he's back as a spirit. And a spirit in itself cannot do a thing in this world except play mind games."

"You think *that* was a mind game?" Logan asked.

"No, no. He's gone beyond being *just* a spirit. He is possessing bodies to do what he wants. Like that man you arrested. That man had no control over what he did. Channing did it all. His spirit possesses people like puppets."

Logan noticed the street vendor smirk as he heard

this. He then walked on with Tess, away from the prying ears.

"You get how nuts this all sounds, don't you?" Logan said in a hushed tone. "You get that this isn't even in the slightest bit logical or believable?"

Tess nodded, looking pensive. "I'm used to it. Been having that my whole life. They called me 'Psycho Seaton' in school, and some still do."

Logan thought for a moment.

"You said he possessed bodies, right?"

She nodded.

"Then, it could be *anyone*, right?"

She nodded again.

Logan motioned to a man sitting on the grass feeding pigeons. "It could be that guy?"

The man, noticing he was being looked at, offered a friendly smile in return. But in this atmosphere, the smile, though friendly and innocent, seemed to Tess to be tinged with a darker malevolence.

"It could be."

"So, he could take control of anyone?"

Three businessmen in suits walked toward them down the path. As they passed, each one of the men looked up and locked eyes with Logan for a second before walking on.

The sound of running feet padded behind them.

"Watch it!" a woman called out.

They moved aside, letting her run past.

As they did, her eyes met with Logan's sternly.

Logan shook off his thoughts. "It could be you?" he asked, staring at her.

She shrugged. "I guess. It's not, though."

"Tess, since this ain't my usual beat, maybe you can fill me in on what the hell I'm supposed to do with all this?"

As he spoke, he struggled to reconcile everything.

Around him, the colors of the plaza played in his vision. He steeled himself as best he could. But in the back of his mind, he could not shake whether the things he had seen had been real or were all part of a hallucination, emboldened by this woman in front of him.

"What do you mean, what are you *supposed* to do?" Tess asked.

"I dunno. Silver bullet? Crucifix? Holy water? Bible verse? Drive a stake through his damn heart?" He was getting exasperated. "What the hell can I do about a ghost trying to use people to kill me?"

"I'm afraid none of that would work," Tess said. "He would jump into another body."

"Are you saying we can't do a thing about it?"

Tess sighed. "To use your vernacular, this ain't exactly my beat either. I spent most of my life telling rich women when they would meet a tall, dark stranger to cheat on their husbands with. Or if a TV series they love may be coming back. Dealing with insanely wealthy people with their insanely inane questions." She shook her head. "So, I'm not an expert in this. In darkness. The *real* darkness out there. I only saw glimpses. I don't understand much of it. And I have read a lot." She paused for a beat. "But I *do* know of a woman. Someone who may be able to help us. I hope she can."

"If she's standing around a cauldron with a big, black pointy hat on, I'm not gonna be so happy," Logan joked weakly, as he felt a shiver of weakness. As his knees started to give way, he grabbed hold of Tess's arm to steady himself.

"What's wrong?"

Logan blinked. The colors in his vision pulsed in rhythm with his heartbeat as it began to throb in his ears.

"I need to sit down," he moaned.

Tess helped him move over to a patch of grass, and they both sat before she asked, "What's wrong?"

Though Logan would never normally speak about this with anyone, especially not someone who may not be sane or someone who could still be part of a Channing cult, he found himself explaining his injury to Tess. What happened that night when Channing stabbed him? The medication. The pain. The colors in his vision. His doubt about what was real.

"In all this," he explained. "Since taking these pills. Pills I've been told can screw with your mind. I've seen some insane stuff. Stuff that can't be real... That *can't*."

Tess understood and empathized. "Not that it makes it any better, but I also saw what you saw in that hotel. I saw that man in a mask... We *both* felt it was Channing, right? We both saw him jump from that building. Even that driver, Randy, did. So, you're not crazy. This was real."

Logan nodded. "But what if, and please don't take offense to this, you're crazy, too?"

Tess couldn't help but smile. "Then, I guess we will both need to be locked up." She motioned to his side. "Do we need to get this looked at if it's hurting that much?"

Logan shook his head. "If I go back to the hospital again, I tell you now that doctor will keep me in. I'll change the bandages. Then we can go see your friend, okay?"

After a few minutes of resting, Tess then helped Logan up, and they then went to flag down a cab.

They traveled back to Logan's apartment, with neither finding the words to describe what they were feeling. Logan, suspecting Tess less and less with each passing second, was stuck in his disbelief that any of this could be real.

Tess respected the silence between them, believing that when they arrived at the convent after his wound was redressed, he may begin to accept the terrifying impossibility she had told him about. That Channing was back.

In the backstreets of Lincoln Heights, the Sisters of the Divine convent had stood for over a century. A large, unassuming compound, it stretched for most of the block it stood on. On the black arched double door, a simple bronze crucifix hung, the only indication of the outside of the religious order that lay beyond its high brick walls.

The door to the convent opened with an aged creak, as a young nun dressed in a long black habit and coif peered out to Logan and Tess. She smiled politely as Tess introduced herself and a more refreshed-looking Logan and explained why they were there and who they wished to see.

After a few minutes of walking through the green, luscious gardens, they then waited in the reception area of the convent. A dark, windowless, wood-paneled area that was claustrophobic and seemed worlds away from the brash Los Angeles streets outside.

Logan watched as the nuns milled by in an almost dreamlike way, their habits hiding their feet, appearing as if they were floating along.

"I'm afraid Sister Marguerite does not normally allow for visitors," an older nun said bluntly as she walked up to them. "Can I ask what this is regarding?"

Taking out his badge, Logan held it up to the nun. "It's police business, ma'am."

The older nun smiled politely yet remained unimpressed. "You can address me as 'Sister,' Detective. And here, the laws of God take precedence over the laws of man, and the folly of your arbitrary rules hold no sway."

Tess shook her head at Logan and then turned to

the nun. "Sister, our visit is more than police business. It's also a spiritual matter of extreme urgency. Urgency I know the sister will want to discuss. Please tell her it is about Transit."

Staring at them, the nun nodded, not knowing what Tess was referring to. "Please wait here." She quietly strolled away down the corridor.

Waiting till she was out of earshot, Tess leaned into Logan and whispered, "I'm surprised you didn't pull your gun on her."

"I won't lie. I considered it."

As they waited, he regarded Tess and, for once, saw her as the woman she was. Even if this was all fairy-tales, she really believed it was true. He always considered himself a good judge of character, his job relied on that. But lately, since he got stabbed, he had been off his game.

Yet standing here, he felt like his old self, perceiving her as an ally, even if a deluded one, but no longer one who had any involvement in any of this. After spending a few hours in her company since the hotel, Logan felt comfortable around her. Even in the silence they shared. This threw into his mind something his father once told him, one of the few things Logan did not understand until right then. *You need to find people you're happy to not speak to.*

He then wondered if she—

"You will be allowed five minutes and not a moment more."

The older nun's voice jolted Logan out of his thoughts and back into the convent.

A dim staircase led down the convent's basement level. The few sconces on the wall, set at equal distances, glowed a yellowness over the reddish brown walls, giving it a very solemn and almost funereal feel.

Along the wall at the far end of this lower-level landing were eight plain-looking brown doors. The older nun motioned to the door on the far left of the room for them to walk to.

Tess nodded as she and Logan followed.

"Tell me how you know of this woman again?" Logan whispered.

"I read about her," Tess replied in an equally quiet voice. "She used to be an exorcist for the diocese. She even wrote some articles on resurrections and demons. I knew she was here but never had enough of a reason to speak to her before."

"And we're sure about her?"

Tess looked back at him with an amused curiosity. "You almost sound nervous, Detective?"

"Face me with a murderer, and I'm cool as a cucumber." Logan glanced around at the shadowed room. "But put me in a dark basement with a load of God stuff, yeah, I'm not at my best."

Tess chuckled, but the nun leading them glanced back with her unamused expression.

"Show some respect," the older nun grimaced quietly as she lightly knocked on the door.

The three small raps echoed around them, a quiet noise that grew seemingly louder in this silence.

With a scraping of metal on wood, the older nun then slid open a viewing panel on the door.

"Five minutes," she reiterated as she turned and shuffled off, back up the staircase, leaving Tess and Logan looking through the panel into a small bedroom.

Inside this cell-like room, statues of Jesus sat on various bits of small and simple furniture, and multiple crucifixes hung from the plain, pale walls. Without a window, a single lit candle was the only light.

Sitting on the edge of the bed in thick shadow, with her back facing them, a habited nun sat in front of the largest crucifix in the room.

"Sister Marguerite?" Tess said through the open panel in the door. "My name is Teresa Seaton, Tess. And I have Detective Russell Logan here."

There was no answer as the nun continued to sit facing away.

"We need your help," Tess continued. "We have heard you have some knowledge of—"

"Transit. I know," she said with a tinge of disdain. "No mortal knows the truth of life beyond ours, if that is what you want to discover." The nun's raspy voice was impassive and stoic. She chose her words carefully. "I have had visitors before who only wished to ask me as if I am the oracle of the afterworlds. Only God, the devil, those above, and those below, truly know what is there."

Tess glanced at Logan, who was staring at the shadowed nun in confusion.

"It is about those below that we're here to ask you about," Tess explained. "You see something that came back. Some*one* came back."

The nun's deep, labored breaths could be heard as the nun took her time to reply. "And this one that came back, how did they die?"

"He was executed," Logan chipped in. "As the states of California and Nevada sentenced him to."

"I have learned it best to let God punish the evil," the nun replied evenly. "Man should have no dominion over a life or the ending of it."

"That's all very good and nice, Sister," Logan said. "But your God didn't do much on this one, so we had to step in and sort it out for him. Or her." He turned to Tess. "Is God he, she, or they?"

"Seriously? You want to ask that now?" Tess replied.

Logan shrugged. "I mean, I know God is called He in some places, but Mother Nature is a She, and She is God as well, right?"

"Your theological pronouns aside," the nun interjected, "God gave life. Man should only accept life and live it till God is ready to take it back."

"Sister," Tess said, focusing on the conversation, "I believe you may be able to help us. Something you once wrote about in an issue of *Sancta Veritas: Catholic Reflections and Scholarship*? Transit?"

"Enough... I have had enough... You must now leave. We have nothing more to speak of. I will not speak to you about things like this."

"Please, Sister Marguerite," Tess implored.

"Transit is an arcane and forbidden concept by the church," the nun said as she stood from the bed. "Let it be."

"I don't mean any disrespect," Logan said, unable to hide his frustration. "But I don't care what the church thinks. People are dying out there, and if you can help, then you'll be saving innocent people's lives. Wouldn't your God want that?"

"Transit is not a toy to be played with," the nun replied as she turned and walked over to the door.

Her face caught in the light for a second, old and haggard, with a grimace multiplying her wrinkles, then she moved the panel slider shut with force.

"Sister Marguerite." Tess banged on the door again.

From down the staircase, the older nun who led them here reappeared.

Logan saw her approach, then turned at Tess. "Come on," he said, walking toward the stairs. "You heard the lady. She can't cut it. Too afraid of what the church would say." After a beat, he muttered, "I think I need a drink, or ten."

Tess, discouraged, looked at the closed door, and they both followed the nun upstairs.

As they left the convent, the daylight had started to

wane, as the city basked in the summer heat.
Everything here was bright, almost too bright. And
with the temperature having broken a hundred degrees
on every street, there were fewer people outside than
usual.

After a walk and a quick taxi ride, Logan made a
beeline for the police precinct parking lot.

Sitting in his and Franklin's police-issue sedan, he
stared at its steering wheel. They were in L.A., there
was no way he could do his job and not drive. Injured
or not, he had little choice but to get his car.

He couldn't be taking taxis and buses to catch a
killer. So, he was lucky he had the car keys because he
would be denied if he tried to sign them out from the
precinct. Lieutenant Grimes would have made sure
that he would not be taking a car until he was signed
fully back to the job. Not that he blamed him for that.
He agreed. But needs must.

He was sitting in the seat Franklin had always
taken, having always been the driver of them. This is
when it hit him again.

The grief. He had witnessed his friend's face be
crushed by the horse's hoof. His head grotesquely
caved in, with his one remaining eye staring up in fear.
Begging for help. Needing to be saved. But Logan
could do nothing for him.

But sitting in the sedan, in the passenger seat,
staring out of the window, he tried his best to hide his
feelings from her. He forced down the lump in his

throat and the tears that threatened to break. Deep down. He had to remain strong and would allow himself time to grieve later. It didn't help that Franklin's destroyed face was the last thing that he had seen of him. Since then, he had a hard time picturing anything else.

"So, you gonna tell me what this Transit is?" he asked Tess, forcing himself to stop dwelling as he started up the engine then drove down Mulholland. "You've been quiet since we left those nuns."

"It's an unholy ritual," Tess replied, sounding deflated. "A way for spirits to use their power to survive death and return to the mortal plane."

"And Marguerite? How does she know anything that can help?"

"She had written papers about it, but I really got to know of her from some old news articles from the sixties that I found. There were a series of murders. All children and babies. The police were hitting a dead end."

"Whoa, are you talking about the Kolfax case?" Logan asked, almost excited. "My commander told me about that years ago. But I looked into it and couldn't find any files on it."

"Erik Kolfax," Tess confirmed with a nod. "They caught that guy, but he wasn't the real killer. He couldn't have been. His crimes matched a previous killing spree a few years earlier. Another child killer called Clive Happs. The new crimes were almost identical to his. And Marguerite believed Happs used Transit to come back. He chose Kolfax to possess, who was not only blind and deaf, but he was also in a wheelchair. Paraplegic. So, for these new crimes, there was no way he could have done it, and the police knew that. But it was Kolfax they found at the scene, up in the third-floor apartment, that had only stairs, holding the knife that was still lodged in that poor kid. Not Happs. The head policeman involved was devout and knew of Marguerite and her research. And after her coming on to help, she believed Happs had come back into Kolfax's crippled body and used him to do these things. The sheer force of Happ's evil superseded any lameness in Kolfax's limbs."

"And everyone died, right?" Logan asked, fascinated.

"Sister Marguerite convinced them to allow Kolfax to be taken into the convent so they could perform the ritual that would send Happs back. But he did not go peacefully. She was the only survivor. The cop died there, too."

Shaking his head, Logan grabbed the pack of cigarettes from inside his jacket.

"Do you mind not smoking?" Tess asked. "It affects me. I mean, it affects what I can do."

"Blocks your hotline to the heavens?"

Tess nodded politely but found that comment hurtful.

Putting the pack back in his jacket, Logan sensed

he may have spoken too harshly. "No disrespect, I dunno what to call it."

"Ability is fine."

They drove for a moment in silence as the car sped along Cahuenga Boulevard.

"So, what's the next hot lead?" Logan asked. "Anyone else know about this stuff? Or should we go get a drink?"

Though he meant the question honestly, Tess took it differently.

"I'm trying, okay? And not like you've come up with any suggestions. Aside from needing a drink. Which you have said three times now."

"Hey, I didn't mean—"

"Pull over."

"What? Come on!"

"I said *pull over*."

Logan slowed the car down and steered over to the edge of the sidewalk. Peering out of his window, he noticed the bright neon sign on the front of the building beside him: *McGuires*. A small neighborhood bar on the street corner.

"I'm thirsty," she said, getting out of the car and then walking straight into the bar.

Logan stared after her, unsure of what happened to get this reaction. Maybe he was not as much on his game as he thought he was.

On instinct, he pulled out his pills from his pocket. He was not in that much pain but still thought about it.

Then the image of Franklin's destroyed face came into his mind, then Carmen's naked, mutilated body, and he could not hold it back. Alone, in the car, he broke down as he wept.

Five minutes later, the door to the bar opened, and Logan stepped in. His eyes were bloodshot, but all other traces of his emotional upset were wiped away, replaced by his steely cop demeanor.

Looking around, he saw the collection of solitary drinkers, who each held onto their glasses of alcohol as if they were fragile, precious gems. Each of them looked more lost in their own depression than the last. The gleam from the neon bar sign reflected on every one of their gaunt faces.

Tess was sitting on a stool at the bar with a half-full glass in her hand and a full one beside it.

As Logan walked up, she glanced around. "You took your time. I got you a scotch." She slid the full glass over to him.

"What are you doing? Trying to prove something?"

"I *need* you to believe me."

"I believe that you believe. Isn't that enough?" Logan replied. "I've no idea what's going on, and you seem to know more than anyone should. And I'm not saying I think you're involved anymore. I can tell you're not. But between you finding me in the hotel and... Wait... that coin thing. That thing you held up to that guy. I forgot about it. What was that?"

Tess sighed as she downed the rest of her glass,

then held it up to the bartender. "Another. And don't water it down this time."

The bartender didn't reply. He looked sheepishly as he refilled her glass straight from the bottle.

"Take it easy," Logan said. "You're drinking like a vice cop."

"Don't worry, I've had lots of practice," Tess replied as she took the second glass and had a sip. "My dad used to put away a bottle a night. I got his genes."

Before Logan could ask her anything else, she sighed and looked at him intently.

"I *need* you to believe me. I know you said you know I believe, but that means nothing in this. Do you want to know how I know? Well, you have to believe me first. Believe that what I am saying is fact and not some baloney I convinced myself of."

Logan didn't answer. He looked guilty. He could not stop his disbelief.

"As for why here?" she continued as she motioned to the bar. "I saw it and knew to come in here. A place to prove something to you. With something you won't want to hear but can't deny." She took another sip. "It was in a place like this your father was murdered, right? Two guys in ski masks. Never knew why they did it, did you?"

Logan's demeanor shifted to one that was much colder as all emotion fell from his face. "I guess you really did your homework." He turned to leave.

"He died for no reason," she said as she grabbed

him by the arm, stopping him from going. "That's when you stopped believing. It made you bitter about Gods and devils and things. It's why no relationships have worked for you."

A sudden anger bubbled up inside of Logan. He hadn't expected anything like this to be said as he stared at her, not knowing where this was coming from.

"But you must believe in *something*. Otherwise, Channing will have the upper hand. You have to believe in *what* he is. But as to why your father was killed, I saw it in a vision when we first met. I know why."

Logan was at a loss.

"It was a rite of acceptance for a gang. They were sent to execute anyone. Just to choose at random and do it. So, those two men, only young boys, really, walked into that bar and did it. No other reason. And the fact there was two of them was not in the press, was it?" Logan shook his head. "But you knew it. And now you know I knew it. So, is that some more proof that maybe what I say could be true? That I can see things? Like how I could know that fact." She took another sip as Logan stared. "So, I want to tell you, please, to keep an open mind. If it is impossible to believe, at least believe that the impossible is a possibility that hasn't happened yet." She took out the silver pentagram amulet from her pocket and slid it over the bar to him. "As for this, it's just a pentagram charm. The star pointing up means ascendance and supremacy of the spirit. The point down, evil, infernalism, and torment. Like up and down."

Logan picked it up and looked it over in his hands. He had seen the figure be enchanted by it when it was held up to him. But could it have been confusion at what she was doing? That seemed a more logical explanation.

"It's not powerful or anything. Only blessed by a priest and symbolic of what Channing is not."

Placing the amulet back on the counter, Logan paused as something occurred to him. "So, are you going to tell me how you knew where I'd be? Did you have a vision of the hotel, too?"

She nodded, then downed the second glass. "I saw you walk into the hotel. I saw you go upstairs. I saw the ax come down." She paused as the words hitched in her throat. "And I saw you die. I saw that ax cut right through you." She turned and looked into Logan's eyes. "Can you imagine what it's like to be haunted by images that not only haven't happened but may never happen? I saw you die. I stopped it. And now I can see you dead on the floor of that dirty hallway, despite it never having happened now? So, you ask me how and why? Well, I don't know. I can feel things, sometimes see them. And, yes, I sell that useless stuff to people.

"But over the past few years, I started seeing and hearing a lot more. As my abilities got better and better, I started seeing more around me. And then I saw the murders. I saw what he did to those people. And I know he saw me watching him, even though I was only having a vision. But that one vision I saw that I called you about? I saw that officer dead. Her head nearly cut off.

"So, I think maybe my vision was not the night you caught him. But the night he killed your colleague afterward. But even then, I had a feeling. A feeling he would come back. So, I told you to make sure he didn't get killed. I told you not to execute him. So, you inadvertently made my vision come true. He would never have taken her if you were not there."

"Are you saying it's my fault?"

"No, not at all. I know what I know and know you can't possibly believe me at my word, but I really needed you too. I don't blame you. But if people *did* believe me, we would not be where we are now. That is a fact."

Logan could not help but sympathize, and his defensive anger abated as he regarded this woman in such obvious torment at what she believed in.

"How about a deal?" Logan asked. "Until I see actual proof of what you say, I will not believe, but I will be ready to believe?"

"That's the best I can hope for, but can I ask something?" Logan paused. "Did you see their faces? The men who killed my dad? Could you pick them out of a lineup?"

"I saw their balaclavas. That's all. I felt them but

didn't see their faces. Besides, they would be a lot older now. Probably not even alive after being in a gang."

Logan looked down at his drink and took a sip. He did not know how to process this.

"Can I ask why you're here? Is it because you are not allowed back on the force full-time because of your injury? You can be honest."

Logan thought for a second. "I guess so. If I was at the station, I would not be allowed to investigate without having a chaperone or being closely moni-tored. But also, and I think more importantly, you have leads, ideas, that no one has thought of. Even if I don't believe them, I have seen some shit I can't explain. I have lost people so dear to me that I owe it to them to exhaust every avenue possible. So, I'm here to see if this has any truth in it."

"I do have an idea. But I'll tell you in the car."

"Where are we going?"

"Burbank."

TRIBULATION

Logan almost pulled the car over as Tess finally told him her plan.

"Why the hell d'you want to go to Channing's house?" he said. "You think 'cause he returned from the grave that he's moved back or something?"

"You know how you have your intuition? Well, mine extends beyond what you can tell about someone from the way they look or act. I can feel deeper things about people. And I know we cannot fight him until we understand more about him. And with his house. I felt it earlier. I know there is *something* there. I don't know how or why, but I know something is waiting for us to see."

As they turned off Sunset Canyon, a dusky haze fell over Los Angeles. Both stared out of the window at the noticeable change in the neighborhoods. Turning down Homburg Street, the houses had gone from nice and respectable to dilapidated and covered in graffiti.

"Is this place abandoned?" Tess asked, staring out at the tagged houses.

"Nah, it's gang country," Logan mused. "Eastside Punks, The Apostles, they all have cook houses here. Methamphetamine brought up from Mexico, turned around here, then dealt on the streets. The tags on the houses are marking their territories."

"If you know they're here, why not arrest them?"

"Bust one, ten more spring up. And the ones that come back always have more guns. They're like vermin, so we just watch them and try to get the people that supply them." Logan looked ahead and spotted a small house clean of graffiti, nestled among the tagged ones. "This is it."

The car pulled up on the curb, and they both got out. They stared at what was quite an eerie structure. With curtains thick and yellowed, the lawn out front was overgrown and with old, rusted kids' toys spread out over them.

"Is she going to know who you are?" Tess asked, not taking her eyes off the house.

"Not unless she saw me on the television. I was in hospital when they searched this place, but... you never know." He took out sunglasses and put them on. "Best hope she isn't great with faces. No way she would let us in if she knew me."

After they rang the bell, the house's front door

cracked open on a chain. An old woman peered out wearing large glasses with coke-bottle lenses, which made her weary, sagging eyes oversized in their magnification. Her hair was pulled back in a very tight bun. Behind her, the house was very dark, shadowed by the closed curtains and low lighting.

Even from where they stood, Logan and Tess could smell the strong, stale odor of dust from within.

"What do you want?" the old woman asked in a low, suspicious tone.

"Evangeline Channing?" Tess said. "We are—"

"From the Herald," Logan said. "We wanted to talk. With the new pentagram murders in the city, we think that maybe it could prove that your grandson, Patrick, was possibly not guilty after all."

The surprise on Evangeline's face was clear, even with the dim lighting.

"We would love it if we could talk to you about this," Tess added.

The door closed, and the chain was then removed.

The inside was unwelcoming. The dark, heavy furniture had all been suffocated under plastic slipcovers. And with the lights all so low, it gave the room a haunted feel. Logan had no option but to remove his sunglasses, as he could hardly see.

"I'm sorry about the light," Evangeline said as she walked over to her couch. "My cataracts restrict me from being able to see well."

"No problem at all, Mrs. Channing," he replied.

Tess stared at the dozens of small ceramic figurines lining every shelf and countertop, each one depicting a child at play.

"Please, sit," Evangeline said.

Evangeline squinted as she stared at Logan. "You look familiar. Are you from this neighborhood?"

"You've probably seen me on the news... I do a lot of on-location stories around L.A.... I even covered your grandson's case. So, you may have caught one of my pieces about him."

Shaking off her suspicion, Evangeline flicked a wave. "So many reporters nowadays. Hard to keep track. Every time I turn on the television, there is a new one there. Younger and younger every day."

Logan laughed. "Now, I can't argue with that. My editor says the same thing almost daily."

"So, you think my Patty could be proved innocent?" Evangeline became more animated as she spoke. "Why didn't you all see the truth earlier? Before you printed all those horrible lies about him?"

"If I'm honest with you, Mrs. Channing, Patri—I mean *Patty*, he didn't help himself in this." The lies were flowing off Logan so naturally Tess couldn't help but wonder why he became a policeman instead of a lawyer or a spy. "You see, he didn't defend himself. He just said he did all those bad things. But one aspect that no one even thought of was that he could have been sick. Needing a psychiatrist instead of a jury."

"And now?" Evangeline asked. "What can be done now?"

"Well, we can't bring him back. But we want to tell the real story. So, he can rest in peace if he is innocent."

Beside Tess, on a small coffee table, stood framed photographs. The one in the middle was an older photo of a man aged in his forties. With a blank expression, he stared directly into the lens.

Picking it up, Tess wondered why the man did not smile.

"That is my husband, Lewis," Evangeline said. "He died too young, though. The good always seem to die young, don't they?"

Evangeline pointed to the frame next to it, showing a teenage girl with the same haunted expression as Lewis. "That one there is our daughter Sarah, Patty's mother," she said somberly. "Died when Patty was only nine. We tried to give him a nice home, but really, he needed a mother. All boys need their mothers."

Tess looked at each photo. None of the subjects in them showed any expression. They all just stared blankly out at her.

"What about his father?" Tess asked, trying to spot anyone it may be among the sea of black-and-white expressionless images.

Evangeline shifted in her seat, looking uncomfortable. "Patty never knew his father."

"That's right," Logan added. "He was illegitimate, wasn't he?"

"No!" Evangeline exclaimed with a sudden, restrained anger. "He wasn't illegitimate. We loved Patty so much. Especially Lewis. He taught him everything he knew. Gave him everything he could. And after Lewis passed, Patty was never the same. We were his parents."

"I'm so sorry for my poor choice of words," Logan said, knowing full well what he was doing and saying.

Pushing the right buttons at the right time. Something he was a master at from all his years of interrogating suspects. Stoking their emotions until they made a mistake.

"I hate to ask, but could we possibly see Patty's room?" he asked. "He did live here some of the time, right?"

"Why on earth would you want to see that?" Evangeline asked.

Logan turned on his full charm. "We want to see the human side of Patty, to show the world his real side. All they know is what the other papers and television have said."

Evangeline nodded. "The filthy police turned the room upside down and inside out. It took me days to get it back exactly as it was. And I have trouble with the stairs. So, I never normally go up there. It was awful. Truly awful how they treated his things."

"I'm so sorry for what you've been through," Logan said.

"Well, I guess you can have a look. What would it hurt, right?" Evangeline's expression fell to sadness. "Not as if people can think any less of my dear sweet boy."

The upstairs hall was lined with bland prints of lifeless landscapes, smiling clowns, and white picket fences. The kind of images that hotels buy in bulk to adorn their rooms.

As Tess followed the grandmother down the hallway, she peered into the open rooms she passed. Each one was pristine. They were so clean they were practically embalmed. Each piece of fabric furniture had been covered in plastic, like downstairs, even the beds.

Getting to the end room, the grandmother opened the door. With cartoony wallpaper and an animal print bedsheet, the room was made up for a child. Not a grown man. There was not a corner that was not stacked high with toys, teddies, puppets, jigsaws, everything to keep a child entertained.

"How often did he stay here?" Logan asked, staring wide-eyed at the young child's room.

"A few days a week," Evangeline replied, staring mournfully. "And I don't care what the papers said. Patty was a happy child. As much as he could have been."

Logan glanced at the grinning teddy bears and other animal faces that peered out from their shelves.

Evangeline continued. "You need to tell them. Tell all of them. Tell the world what a good boy he was. He was quiet and considerate. Not this monster they want him to be. Murder? What nonsense. You only had to speak to him to see his angelic nature."

Tess, meanwhile, was not listening. She stared at the brass framed bed, at the child's music box that sat on the side table. Her eyes started to feel itchy, and her skin became littered with gooseflesh as her focus intensified toward the box.

Quietly, she stepped over to it, almost in a trance. Picking it up, she wound up the crank on the box's side. Then a haunting nursery melody began to play.

The grandmother looked over happily, remembering the music box's song all too well.

The tinkling, tinny tune was hypnotic as it played.

Tess's expression then fell. "He used to... to come... in here... every night... Whisky... Whisky. He stank of whisky."

Her voice seemed very far away. Her eyes were unfocused as they stared down at the box in her hands, as if she was looking through it and into something else.

Then her whole body spasmed.

She dropped the music box and held her hands over her ears, drowning out an agonizing sound that no one else in the room could hear.

"No!" she screamed out in a high-pitched child's voice, a voice that sounded more akin to a young boy, not like her. "No, Grandpa, please! Not again! Grammy, grammy, make him stop. Please, Grandpa, stop!"

Evangeline turned white with shock, recognizing the voice. "Patty? What is this? What are you doing?"

Logan rushed to Tess's side. Realizing what was happening but not understanding how or why. "Patrick?"

"Grampa, leave Mommy alone!" the childlike voice cried from Tess's lips.

"Is he hurting her?" Logan asked.

His belief in what was happening grew by the second.

"Grandpa, please stop doing that to her!" the voice cried again as tears streamed down her face. "Oh, no... Not me... Please, Grandpa! I said I'd be good. Please, no! It hurts so much. Grammy, Grammy! *Help, he's hurting me!*"

Logan shot Evangeline a shocked look. "You were *there?*"

"I don't know what you are saying," Evangeline said, agonized.

"He molested his own daughter *and* Patrick, and you *knew?*" Logan couldn't hide his revulsion as something clicked. "Wait... Patrick's father? It was his grandfather, wasn't it? *Wasn't it?*"

Tess, still in a trance, bolted for the door.

Evangeline's eyes blazed with anger as her upset

gave way. She stared back at Logan. "*I know you!* You're no reporter. You are *him. You're him!* That filthy cop. You murdered my Patty!"

Logan just left, down the stairs, through the kitchen, and into the backyard.

Evangeline's furious screams could be heard from upstairs. "You are a *murderer!* Eternal punishment awaits you! *Burn in hell! Burn in hell!*"

Outside, the night had begun to take over, killing off all the light it could find, smothering it till morning.

Tess sprinted across the yard at a frantic pace. Logan struggled to keep an eye on her as he tried to keep up. He could, though, clearly hear her childlike cries.

"*No, Grampa, no!*"

He followed through a break in the fence at the end of the yard into a cluster of trees. He had to move slowly, as he was unable to see where he was stepping, so he trod carefully as he followed Tess's cries.

His mind raced with what had happened. He knew that what he said, what he heard was outlandish and out of the realms of his sanity. But he believed somehow, he knew every word he heard was real, that she *was* Patrick. Somehow.

Ahead, the trees opened into a steep incline, down to the fenced-off concrete basin of the Los Angeles reservoir. Streetlights from the road on the other side shone down, illuminating its gray concrete.

As if she had been there before, Tess scrambled through a small break in the chain link, still sobbing in young Patrick's voice.

"*It hurts!*" she screamed.

Logan followed as fast as he could, one hand holding his bandaged stomach as he moved, his eyes not leaving her.

Down the concrete basin, one of the sloping walls gave way to a spillway tunnel leading back under the ground. Tess ran into the darkness within without a pause for thought.

Logan followed soon after, but as he did, he slipped on the water-slicked ground beneath him, only managing to stay upright. He frantically grabbed his lighter from his jacket, flicked it open, and sparked the flame to life. Casting the spillway's thick blackness aside.

In the nine-foot-wide tunnel, the ground beneath him slanted down as water trickled down its middle, disappearing ahead. The smell of rust and mold was so strong it was almost unbearable.

Tess could not be seen or could no longer be heard, as Logan moved forward at a determined pace.

The tunnel soon ended at a large metal door. The bottom of which had been bent upward, big enough to crouch in. Without hesitation, he scrambled through.

On the other side, it opened into a much larger area, where rusted pipes and wheels lined the walls in a mass of conduits that fed the water away in various directions. Tess stood in front of a small rectangular doorway leading into more darkness beyond.

"Hey," Logan called out as he got closer. "What's down here? What do you see?"

Tess, disorientated, did not answer. She kept staring ahead into the shadows. The tears that had flooded her cheeks were drying up, leaving salt tracks on her skin.

"Hey, you!" a voice shouted out from behind as a flashlight shined over them.

Logan grabbed the hilt of his gun on his belt as he turned. Expecting to see Channing standing there. But instead, it was a uniformed worker with a yellow hard hat on his head, a big beard resting on his barreled chest.

Tess was still in her trance as Logan squinted into the man's light.

"What the hell do you think you're doing down here?"

The workman demanded to know as he turned his flashlight to the ground, out of Logan's eyes.

Releasing the hilt, Logan opened his jacket and showed off the LAPD badge clipped onto it. "Police."

"Don't care if you're the king of Siam. You can't be down here. It's not safe."

Logan nodded. "What is this place?"

"Part of the old city's water system. They shut it down after the quake in '71." The workman shone his torch over the surrounding walls. As he did so, the light exposed what Logan's lighter could not see: the multitude of cracks over the concrete. "All these tunnels and storm drains go on for miles, and all are broken up. They could collapse at the smallest of things."

Without listening, Tess reached up to a vertical pipe beside her, and her fingers touched the rusted wheel on it.

"Hey, lady," the workman called out urgently. "Don't touch that. Or anything. These pipes are still full of water. You open that, it could start a chain reaction and flood this place." He then pointed his torch to the dark opening ahead of them. "And down there? A kid drowned a few years back after thinking they could just walk around. All this system should have been bricked up after that. But the city thinks it's too expensive. You're lucky I saw you come in here."

Logan turned at the opening, then back to the workman. "Patrick Channing used to come down here a lot, right? To these tunnels?"

"Not again." He sighed in annoyance. "That was before I was assigned to this section. I've been in Pasadena for the last six years." The workman then took a step forward. "Now, come on. You both gotta leave. Right now!"

Tess then lurched forward as her whole body began to shake. She grimaced in pain as she clenched her fists. Screaming as she lifted them upward.

"What the hell's goin' on with her?" the workman

asked as he then noticed the blood that began to drip out between her fingers.

"Tess!" Logan shouted as he grabbed her by her shoulders, steadying her shaking body.

Sluggishly, she opened her eyes. In the flashlight, they all could see it. On the palms of her hands, like stigmata, two pentagrams, pointed down, were etched in blood.

"H-He's so angry," Tess muttered, her voice hers again. "He's mad we came here. This is *his* place. The only place he felt safe. He spent all his time here. Practicing everything."

The worker stared at her palms caught in his flashlight beam, not registering what she was saying, shocked.

Tess's eyes then widened as she took in a deep gasp. Her vision faded and was replaced with something else. Something far away that made her wretch, then collapse against Logan, who grabbed onto her tighter.

"He's now laughing at us... He's going to kill again... A building with a high chimney." She gasped as the agony then left her body as soon as it arrived.

As she lifted her palms again, all three could see that the carved pentagrams were gone, as if they were never there.

"It's okay," Logan said, unsure of what could help.

Tess looked up at him, terrified. "I heard his voice. He spoke to me as he murdered them. Spoke to *both of us* as if we were standing right there. It's a trap. He wants us to go to where he is."

They left the tunnels, leaving the worker standing there, bewildered and freaked out. Logan had one arm around Tess as he hurried her back to the sedan, avoiding Evangeline Channing's house as much as they could.

"So, what did you hear, exactly?" Logan asked as they both sat in the car with the ignition off.

"He said..." She swallowed nervously. "'Come and get me, buddy boy. And bring that whore, too.'"

She almost burst into floods of tears. Her voice quivered under the emotional strain.

Logan stared forward. "Huh. Well, I guess between that and what I saw on your hands. What happened in the room... I guess. I guess... I... I believe you." He looked at her. "If I hadn't seen all this, I could have said it points to you being in league with him."

Tess went to answer, but Logan interrupted any protest. "But more than all that. I told no one that he called me buddy boy. No one. And he called me it quite a few times. So, I know at least he told you that, whether in that vision, or in cahoots. But your hands... those star things." He shook his head as he could hardly believe his words. "It means you're not only believing what you say, but it's enough evidence for me to believe as well. Even though when you say it aloud, it all sounds *totally* looney tunes."

Tess nodded as she looked at her healed hands. "I

don't know what it meant." She examined her untouched palms. "I felt the knife cutting into my skin. I felt him carving in them as he laughed." She shivered.

"What about the rest of it?" Logan asked as he turned over the ignition. "You got any more to go on than a high chimney?"

"I didn't see who he was killing. I only knew it was someone close to you. I could feel it. Everything he has done since coming back seems to be so personal to you. *Aimed* at you. But not so much in a blaming-you-revenge type thing. He's not sad he's dead. He's glad. He has the power he wants. But I can feel that all he wants now is to play with you... Maybe we shouldn't go. If he knows we are coming."

"I don't think we have a choice, do we?" he said, switching the headlights on.

"I suppose. All I know is that it's in a factory or something with a high chimney."

"Like those off the Santa Monica Freeway?"

Logan was processing everything. Trying to work it out logically.

"So, is this a Catholic thing?" he asked.

"No, it's much older than all that. Churches preserved older, arcane beliefs into their history. Whereas science discarded them as made-up superstitions. Like with Transit some Abrahamic religions called it the First Power. The power to come back. More than mere resurrection. The bible is littered with those. Jesus, Lazarus of Bethany, Tabitha. But they soon discovered more about it, that dead souls could come back and take hold of the living. Sister Marguerite read lots of forgotten texts and saw Transit as not solely a power of the saints, as some theologians had theorized. But was a power for the darkness. A power of hate. Beyond any new god."

She took a breath as she noticed that Logan was listening intently to her, hanging on her every word.

She continued. "As for the pentagram. That's older than the church, too. But Christians adopted it and slightly altered its meaning to suit their needs. They say it symbolizes the five wounds of Christ, his hands and feet punctured by the crucifixion, and his side pierced by a soldier's spear, or they say it's the star of Bethlehem. And upside down, they say it's the antithesis of Christ. Like the two points to them looked like devil horns."

"Like the antichrist? They do that with crosses, too, right? Upside down means evil."

Tess nodded. "But long before Catholicism rebranded it with its own meaning, it meant up and down depending on which way its pointed. All opposites. Light and dark. Good and evil. But with Channing. He used the pentagram to identify his actions. He imbued that symbol with power, through blood. Though, I think he probably sees it as a sacrifice to a higher power. He *made* the symbol a part of him so the reverse of the symbol is as powerful to him, it's why it worked to hold him for a second back in the hotel. Not that I knew it would. It was a swing in the dark."

"What do you think he believes? In the devil?"

"Yeah, I think he does. In the bits I've been able to see about him, he alluded to it, right? And the murders were all positioned and done in a specific way as described in lots of demonology books he had, well, that's what the press said."

"Yeah, almost to a T, each one. Down to the number of candles, position of the body, and wounds. Everything was a copy from various things we found in his shack. Like he picked and chose bits from all over the place."

"I don't think he really knew where the power came from, at least I'm not sure how he did. No one alive can. But I think it was all happenstances. He happened to believe in things that enabled Transit without totally understanding it. Whereas now? Now, he will know everything about it as he has seen beyond death. He probably now thinks of what he believed before as being foolish."

"And what do we do to beat him?" Logan asked, hopeful.

"I-I don't know, but if you kill the body he's in, that innocent person dies. Maybe if they die quickly, his spirit won't have a chance to jump and could die with them? Or if he is just trapped?"

"That coin thing, that could hold him while I put him down, right?" As he spoke, Logan did not like what he proposed. It would still be an innocent person he would have to shoot, whether being forced to do those awful things. "I guess all I can hope is that we stop what he is planning tonight and try to figure out how to beat him tomorrow."

"That's if it's tonight," Tess added. "Remember before, it was a couple of days after the vision that he appeared? That's if that vision was that one. Or the one where your friend died. Hell, for all I know, me telling you all of this could be the reason any of it happened. Like a self-fulfilling prophecy."

Past the throb of the downtown nightlife, the sedan then turned off an exit on the Santa Monica Freeway and toward the industrial part of town. Toward factories with high chimneys.

Through an elevated part of the freeway, Tess had her eyes closed as she tried to feel the way for them to go. Logan drove forward, peering at her occasionally, waiting for her signal.

He felt a bit foolish being here, as if they were right. How the hell could he think to beat someone like Channing? If they were wrong, then they were going further down the rabbit hole of a possible joint delusion. It was then he considered his meds again. His injury. The doctor's warning of opioid-induced hallucinations and paranoia.

"Next right," she blurted out, her eyes opening to see the road ahead.

Without questioning, he approached a four-way

intersection and turned the sedan right, only to be confronted with a dead end about fifty meters ahead of them.

"No, wait." Tess looked around, confused. "It could be left... Or straight ahead? Actually, go straight ahead. Yeah." She kept looking around, trying to find a familiar clue from her vision.

Logan turned the car around and drove back on his original route.

Grabbing her handbag, Tess started to root around it.

"What're you looking for?"

"Things to use against Channing if we see him," she said, pulling out a small lavender-tinted crystal. "Some people say violet stones are effective for controlling entities from lower planes."

Logan smiled. "Well, I have a double barrel in the back, which is what I'll rely on."

His gallows humor was one of the few things that stopped him from turning and leaving. Feeling so far out of his depth.

"Wait, *was* it left back there?" Tess said. "I can feel it. This is *not* where we should be... Or maybe it was right. Damn!"

The radio buzzed with static. "All units. Code Three. 9534 Julian Street, near Alameda. All units. Code Three. Respond."

"That means officer down," Logan said as he slammed on the brakes and turned around. "It *was* left.

It's only a few blocks away," he said as he reached for the radio mic. "Three Lincoln forty-three, I'm on it."

Grabbing a police light from under his seat, he opened the window, then attached the light's magnetized base to the car's roof. Within a moment, the siren was wailing, and the red light flashed as they sped toward Julian Street.

CONVERGENCE

Julian Street was a wide avenue with large decrepit warehouses on either side. Old and rotten shells of forgotten businesses. Vestiges of yesteryear. The empty mills and factories had been left derelict for years, stuck in contract hell between the city and developers. It was a collection of abandoned structures that, under the glow of the streetlights and bright moonlight, seemed ghostly. Their crumbling walls, silhouetted catwalks, not to mention the copious amounts of graffiti tags that overlapped each other on every reachable surface. These buildings were the homes for vagrants, rats, and junkies.

"Wait here," Logan said as he got out of the sedan and grabbed the shotgun and flashlight from the trunk.

Tess, still in the passenger seat, stared helplessly up at the building numbered 9534. She watched as Logan disappeared into an open doorway.

The radio crackled again. "Code three... All units. Code three, officer in trouble. Respond," the dispatcher repeated.

Tess looked worriedly at the looming structure, but her attention was ripped back to the radio as the dispatcher began to laugh. A chilling laugh. A familiar laugh. The hair on her neck stood on end as she drew in a breath.

"But you know which officer needs the help the most, eh, sugar tits?" the dispatcher gleefully said, as his voice then dropped all pretense. "Ol' buddy boy, Russell Logan. Supercop."

Channing giggled before the radio went dead.

Inside the warehouse, it was a labyrinth of cracked walls, corridors that had been blocked with debris, and collapsed staircases. Even parts of the ceiling had buckled downward, exposing the next floor above it through the holes. Pockets of light from the street lamps broke through all available windows and cracks, dotting orange rays over the wrecked area where Logan stood. He had his at the ready and his flashlight shining ahead of him. The light shimmered across all the broken glass on the uneven floor.

"Logan," Tess called out as she ran into the warehouse's doorway, leaving the sedan wide open.

She had no gun or no light.

Inside, the darkness hit her hard as the corridor she soon found herself in was devoid of any windows and kept the darkness in tightly. She looked around desperately as she called out again, "Logan?"

Further in, the shadows become so thick that nothing could be seen ahead of her. As she stared, she started to wonder if Channing was standing there, masked by the shadow, in front of her, waiting to strike.

"Logan," she called out again, her voice more panicked, echoing off the walls.

A hand thrust out from the darkness behind her and grabbed her by the arm. She screamed as she turned to see the annoyed face of Logan lit up by the brightness of his flashlight.

"I told you to *stay* in the car," he admonished. "It's not safe here."

"It's him," Tess said in a panic. "I heard him on the radio. It was Channing. This *is* a trap! He is waiting."

"Doesn't mean we can't stop him, though."

"You don't understand. I get what I saw in my vision now. *You* are the next victim. *You* are the one I saw him kill. You have to leave here now!"

"No. Tess, you have to leave," Logan said as he kept an eye on his surroundings. "I'm trained for this stuff. You're a civilian. You cannot be here. I have to be. I don't have a choice in it. I started this. I gotta finish it."

Echoing in the darkness was a laugh.

That laugh.

Channing's laugh.

"Oh, Logan, sweet Logan," the voice said, sounding far down the dark corridor ahead.

Logan let go of Tess and aimed his shotgun and torch to where the voice came from. His expression was fixed like a hunter, whereas all traces of bravado evaporated out of Tess in an instant.

"You want to protect her, don't you?" Channing added. This time, his voice had come from behind them. "I will make her watch me kill you... Then I'll skin her from head to toe."

Logan spun his aim behind them.

Channing's laugh echoed out again, this time from all around them.

On instinct, Logan turned and took off down the corridor toward where the laughter seemed to disappear.

"You need to go!" he called back to Tess.

But she was not listening. She followed Logan, feeling guilty for bringing him here, to what she saw as his execution. An execution that may never have happened if she hadn't told him about her vision.

Rushing up a flight of rotten wooden stairs, the darkness abated as the light from outside seeped into the windowed corridor.

"I'm so happy you are here, buddy boy."

His voice sounded so close yet so far at the same time without any discernable direction.

As they walked through darkened turns, the crumbling floor beneath them cracked with each step they took.

Just as Logan had started to wonder if this was in

his head again, a silhouette appeared on the wall far in front of them. A distorted huge shadow where the corridor opened into a large hollow chamber.

As Logan saw the shadow, he raised the shotgun and fired ahead. Not leaving anything to chance and being not inclined to ask questions first. The shot ricocheted off a wall as the shadow of the figure slunk away unscathed.

Peeking around the room, with his shotgun tracing his gaze, Logan controlled his breath, focusing on his surroundings.

"What if I'm only in your mind?" Channing said. "You know she could just be feeding your delusions, right?"

"That's not true," Tess whispered, afraid.

"Over here," Channing said, his voice from the left.

Logan turned his aim as he stepped forward.

Channing's voice shifted to the far side of the room. "How about over here?"

Logan crept forward, shotgun always first.

"And here?" Channing added again, his voice turning Logan's path to the left.

He hadn't known it, but the voice had led him to a certain place in the room.

As Logan stepped forward a few spaces, the floor beneath him cracked inward. Breaking apart under his weight. Plunging him downwards into the darkness and slamming him hard onto the concrete floor, laying over twenty feet below.

As he landed with a thud and a groan, his shotgun went off, blasting against a nearby wall. His flashlight smashed into the ground beside him, its beam cutting off.

Frantically, Tess stared down into the hole, unable to see anything in the darkness below. "Logan!"

He did not reply. She could only hear his whimper.

She grabbed the lavender-tinted crystal from her pocket and gripped it defensively.

"What a pretty rock," the voice from behind her said.

Tess gasped. The dark figure stood a few feet behind her, wearing the same translucent smiling mask it wore in the hotel.

"Stand back!" she screamed and turned, holding the crystal up at him.

With a snicker, the figure was then closer to her. He slapped the crystal from her hand, sending it to the ground, where it shattered into tiny shards.

"So fragile," the figure giggled. "Like bones. So damn easy to crack, so difficult to put back together."

As Tess stared at him, she could see it was not Channing inside. Despite his voice, his eyes were not the same as the photos she had seen or the man she had seen in her visions.

Grabbing the pentagram amulet from her pocket, she held it up.

"You think that will work again?" the figure said in

amusement. "It's sweet that you think it might, but it was only a parlor trick. Nothing more."

Despite her intense fear, she stared into the figure's eyes. Eyes of this much older man. Not the eyes of the killer within him. But she was battling the spirit of the monster, not the vehicle.

"You can't keep killing people forever, Patrick," she said as she backed away toward the rotten staircase.

"By the very nature of what I am, I think you're mistaken," the figure replied with a sadistic tone. "I can kill until the last drop of innocent blood is spilled."

He then bolted forward, lunging at her, but Tess managed to escape into the darkness of the adjacent corridor but as she did—

She ran right into the masked figure's arms, who had impossibly appeared in front of her.

Yelling, she kicked her way out of the figure's grasp and stumbled back the way she came—

But it stood in her path, the figure. Yet again.

Backing up against the nearby wall, she looked desperate while the figure regarded her.

A small chuckle escaped his lips.

She noticed a metal ladder affixed to the opposite wall, leading upward. As fast as she could, she raced over and scrambled up the metal rungs, not even looking behind her. Higher and higher, she climbed up to a metal catwalk that laced around the top of the second-story factory floor.

Behind her, a *clank, clank, clank* reverberated heavy footsteps on the ladder.

Getting closer.

Faster.

As she clambered onto the catwalk, the metal footway led in either direction. She had no time to do anything except arbitrarily choose which way to go and hope it was the right choice.

Dazed, with a twisted ankle and a wound aching intensely, Logan managed to get to his feet. From the darkened room he had landed in, he peered upward with a pained wheeze and could see Tess, very high above, running down the metal catwalk, closely followed by the figure, who was walking behind her in pursuit slowly. The long-serrated knife dangled in his hand glinted in the reflected streetlight.

Hurriedly, Logan saw his broken flashlight and grabbed his shotgun. He raced back up the rotten staircase, every part of his body crying out in pain with each step. He grunted and groaned as he forced himself up the metal ladder after them.

Tess ran as fast as she could along the walkway, not daring to look down into the cavernous factory floor below. But then her heart sank, and her fear rose as the walkway ended abruptly. Her escape path was no longer a possibility.

Turning, she expected to see the figure right upon her. Instead, he was standing about twenty feet away, turned away, staring at Logan, who hobbled up the metal ladder onto the catwalk.

"Buddy boy!" the figure shouted as it raised the blade high.

With a swift motion, Logan brought the shotgun up and fired it into the chest of the man, who staggered backward. But this didn't stop him.

In a flash, he was in front of Logan, kicking the shotgun from his hand, sending it clanging to the catwalk's floor. Then, with incredible agility, the figure leaped into the air and, while coming down, punched Logan in the top of his skull, sending him crumpling to the walkway.

Dazed, Logan could see his shotgun blurred in front of him, but before he could reach for it, a large work boot slammed into his gut against his bandage.

Logan could feel his stitches rip as he let out a terrible cry of agony.

His boot then turned and kicked Logan in the face. A loud crunch echoed through Logan's ears as his nose broke. A searing pain shot across his skull as his nostrils burst with blood.

Trying to crawl to his feet, Logan's eyes were drenched in tears and blood as he tried to focus through his pain. But the figure was soon on him again, ready to kick him through the bars of the catwalk and down the fifty-foot drop to the concrete below.

"Hey, asshole!" Tess screamed.

Before the figure could turn to see the sudden

oncoming assault, Tess jumped toward him. Her long nails, out like talons, raked at his eyes through the wide slits of the mask.

He tried to push her back, but his boots got caught on Logan, who was still on the floor, trying to get to his feet.

Tess's nails scratched in his eye and sliced through something wet and soft.

The figure growled in anger as he fell backward, tumbling off the catwalk. Down onto a mass of cracked and jagged concrete that lay in front of the loading dock shutter. Onto pieces of wall that had fallen there in a solid heap.

As the figure collided, his throat erupted in a torrent of blood, and his spine and neck snapped. His head twisted into a terrifying angle as his leg bones tore through the flesh, splitting out through the fabric of his trousers.

Within a matter of moments, the figure's breathing got shallower as his broken body became still. The torrential jets of blood pulsed slower and slower as he bled out. Dying in seconds.

Up on the catwalk, Tess held Logan up as they peered over the side at the scene.

"I have to see," Logan muttered, and he staggered back to the ladder, holding his shotgun loosely.

The climb down was slow and painful. Logan could feel the warmth of the blood drenching his midriff and the pain from his nose, ribs, and the rest of his body almost broke him.

But he had to persist. He *had* to see the man under the mask. He knew it could not be the face of Channing, but he had to see who it was under there. Not that it would make any difference who it may have been, could have been another junkie.

Tess wanted to leave, to run, but she was too much in shock to process any of this. Her actions had scared her. Trembling, her momentary rage had since dissipated, leaving her worried about what she may be capable of. She still felt the wetness of blood under her fingernails, and the thought of what she had done made her feel sick.

Down in front of the loading dock shutter, light from outside, a mix of moonbeam and street lamp, shone onto the still body of the figure, contorted and twisted. Draped over the jagged rock.

Getting closer, Logan and Tess walked separately as they stared at the man. Logan was slow and hobbling along and about ten paces behind. Tess reached forward with a nervous hand and grabbed the translucent mask by its edges. She pulled it off, exposing his face.

She was met with the visage of Patrick Channing. One of his eyes had been clawed out. He looked directly at her with a wide, terrifying grin. She screamed as she glanced away in horror.

Logan staggered up. "It's okay. He can't hurt you." He peered down at the man's face.

It was not Patrick Channing who looked up with one burst eyeball. It was the lifeless body of Lieutenant Jonah Grimes, who stared up at him.

If Logan didn't know better, he could have sworn he heard a laugh in the distance.

Within the next two hours, the warehouse was crawling with police officers, forensic staff, and detectives. A whole crew of people called in from their downtime in the middle of the night.

Two officers had outlined the dead body of Lieutenant Grimes, still draped in a heap over the concrete, as photographs were being taken.

Outside the warehouse, Logan, bruised with a plaster over his nose, his side re-bandaged up, stood next to Commander Perkins. They both watched the crime scene through the open loading dock door. Tess stood a few feet behind them, looking unsure and scared.

"Some guy lures you here, dressed up like Patrick Channing and..." Perkins said, hardly believing his own words. "And it's Jonah Grimes?" He turned at Logan with a mixture of suspicion and disbelief. "Are you really saying that's what happened?"

"Yeah," Logan answered, still in shock from what happened. "I know how it sounds. Sounds more plausible that I led him down here, dressed him up, and threw him off the catwalk, right?"

The pain in his body was still throbbing but a lot less than it had been. The meds the EMT medic gave him were stronger than his prescribed ones and were taking hold. His burst stitches were cleaned and held closed with tape. A temporary measure before he had to go to the hospital.

"Sounds better than what you're telling me." Perkins' accusing glare stayed on him. "Sure, Grimes was a drunk and a rude prick, but he was also one of us. And I can't believe he went doolally insane. You hated him. That's a major suspicion of foul play. You know that, right?"

Before Logan could reply, Perkins noticed a large SUV driving up through the police cordon. He sighed. "*Of course* the damn commissioner has to show up." He was getting angrier by the second. "I warned you to back off. I *told you* that you're burned out! If there is a shit storm heading this way, you better tell me anything else you are hiding, Russ. Right now."

"I gotta ask you about Erik Kolfax and the people that died?" Logan asked.

Perkins was a man used to taking a blow and not flinching, having been in the political firing line for a decade. His poker face was second to none.

But he looked like he had been punched heavily in the gut.

"I told you to never speak about that!" Perkins chided, speaking under his breath so Tess couldn't hear. "It was taken off the books for a reason. I was told to back away from the highest level."

"Well, Tess knew about it," Logan said, motioning to her. "And she thinks these crimes are connected. Happs came back, then..."

"What has *that* got to do with *this*? Erik Kolfax is as dead as Patrick Channing, and beyond that, there is nothing similar. That's superstitious nonsense!"

A uniformed officer walked over to them. "Commander Perkins? The commissioner wants to speak to you. The press are going nuts. He wants you over there now."

"Please," Logan cut in, keeping eye contact with Perkins. "You know me. You know I didn't do anything. Even if you can't quite believe what I said, you know I wouldn't have done this. Please, give me some more time to prove it."

"Sir," Tess spoke up, unsure of how to address Perkins. "What he said was exactly what happened. That man did all this, and we stopped him. I know he was a policeman, but it doesn't change the facts."

She knew she was a bad liar, but she wouldn't mention that Channing did this. That was what they agreed to say. She and Logan had both agreed to leave any talk of Transit out of the conversation. Grimes lived alone, had no family. Blaming him alone was awful, but it was better than the alternative of being branded insane.

Of course, Perkins knew Logan could not have

done this, but he also could not fathom that Grimes did that to Franklin and Carmen.

"We'll run prints on the crime scenes so far and compare them to Grimes," Perkins sighed. "I'll hold off on the press conference until that's done, and I'll get the commissioner to wait somehow. But I'm not condemning him until we have evidence beyond an overly medicated officer's word. Got it?"

Logan stared at him in surprise. Was his condition that obvious to Perkins? It must have been, but Logan had no idea.

Perkins motioned to the other side of the building behind them. "Go out back. I don't want the commissioner asking you anything, okay?"

Logan smiled in thanks, but Perkins could not manage one in return.

————

Back at Logan's apartment, as daylight broke, he and Tess sat in his sparse living room. Forgoing the hospital, he had opted to try to solve this first before being lectured by his doctor again.

Jack had hidden in the bedroom, wary of the stranger sitting in his space on the couch, grumpily sulking beside the dresser.

In the living room, Tess tried to ignore the stale smell of cigarettes that permeated every surface and clung to the back of her throat.

"Is that it? Is it over?" Logan asked.

"I don't know." Tess shrugged. "I really don't. I've exhausted my abilities on that. Unless a vision comes, I'm stuck. Maybe he has gone off to find another vessel. Or that body could have died too fast to escape from?"

"We gotta pray that Grimes's fingerprints give him away and clear any suspicion on me."

"And if not?"

Logan shook his head. "I gotta plead my case. It's hard to believe, but it's not a lie. Channing used Grimes to kill. It was Grimes's hand that did it. We're just leaving out the ghost stuff."

"He may have used someone else before, and only recently took control of Grimes," Tess mused. "Grimes may have not killed anyone."

"I hate to say it, but I hope to hell he did."

"Also, why did you bring up Erik Kolfax?"

"I always thought Perkins may have had more to do with it, and after what you told me... Maybe he was already a believer who could help." Logan considered taking out a cigarette, but judging by Tess's past reactions, he dismissed the idea. "And from what Perkins said when I asked, I doubt he knew much of the truth of it. And I doubt he would have helped us get through to that nun again."

Logan moved beside her and put a hand on her knee. "We will get through it, though. I'll make sure none of this thing falls on you."

But as his hand connected with her, she glared into his eyes as her expression fell. A fear seeped over her.

"No," she mouthed.

Concerned, Logan removed his hand. "You got that look on your face. What did you see?"

Tess couldn't answer and just looked more scared by the second.

"You saw something, didn't you?"

Tess stood and began pacing, trying to shut the images she saw out of her head.

"Tess, please! Did you see me die again?"

She shook her head, a wealth of embarrassment on her face.

"What is it?"

"You really wanna know?" Before waiting for a reply, she blurted, "I saw you and me together!"

Logan did not expect that.

She started to babble. "But what I see doesn't always happen. It's only a possibility. I mean... Oh God, what am I saying? I—"

A scratching sound came from down the hallway, stealing both of their attentions away from her unexpected confession.

"Jack's probably clawing at the bed again," he said, shaking his head as he achingly stood. "Little asshole would destroy everything in this apartment if he could. Love that little guy, though." He walked toward the bedroom, amused. "One sec, and you're gonna tell me everything about what you saw."

After he walked out of the room, a sudden tapping from the window behind her made Tess snap her attention backward. Staring at the clear glass, she saw nothing there. Not that there should be anything, as it was a four-story window with no fire escape near to it.

Shaking it off, she turned back, but as soon as she did, another tapping sounded from the glass.

Cautiously and against every fiber in her body telling her otherwise, Tess stood and walked toward the tapping.

Her blood ran cold as, moving into view, staring back at her, the toothless grin of an old vagrant lady stared back at her. Leering, chuckling to herself, as she clung to the window frame.

Then, with a banshee's wail, this bag lady punched at the window, breaking it with a loud crash.

Tess fell backward in shock, knocking over the lamp, which shattered on the floor. Its porcelain base in pieces among broken window shards.

The old lady climbed in, cackling.

"Russell!" Tess screamed in terror.

"What is it?" Logan asked, crouching beside her.

With her eyes squeezed shut, she then pointed to the window.

Logan looked. Everything seemed normal. No broken window. Nothing out of the ordinary. Aside from the shattered lamp on the floor.

"She was there," Tess whimpered.

"Who?"

"I don't know. Some kind of filthy old woman."

Logan stared at the window, then back to Tess. "Four stories up?"

"I know how it sounds."

Shaking his head, Logan stood and walked over to the window, reaching to open it.

In a split second, the window crashed inward, and the old bag lady smashed her way inside. She crashed into Logan, sending him to the floor as she landed on top of him.

Tess recoiled in terror.

The old lady's foul-smelling, pockmarked face leaned in closely to Logan. "Do you think I'm pretty, buddy boy?" Channing said from her gummy, rancid mouth. As he grinned maniacally at him, a string of browning drool seeped from her gums and onto his face.

Without a pause, Logan smashed his forehead hard into the lady's round, sagging face. And even though this force was immense, her expression didn't change as he headbutted, as if something lighter than the breeze had drifted past her skin.

"It's not nice to hit a lady, Logan," the old lady said. "Didn't your mom teach you that?"

With all his strength, Logan managed to kick the old woman off as he got to his feet. He grabbed Tess as he made a beeline for the front door.

"Oh, goodie," the bag lady said. "I love a good game

of hide and seek... I'm *it*. I'll count from ten." She paused until the door opened. "Ten!"

Tess and Logan raced down the stairs. Logan tried to get the wind back in his lungs.

"Nine, eight, seven," the old lady cried out from the apartment above.

They pounded down the stairs toward the garage. Logan did not even consider fighting back anymore. He thought he could lure this woman out in public so there would be lots of witnesses to see what was happening.

As they arrived at the parking garage and into his car, they could not hear the old woman.

"Ready or not, here I come," she screamed from high above.

The sedan raced out of the apartment and into the early morning city. The sun rose higher in the sky as the people began to wake up to another hot, humid day.

Logan turned onto the freeway overpass, intent on getting to the precinct as fast as he could, or at least as far from his apartment as possible.

Jack! He could not believe he had left Jack there. Hopefully, the old woman left in pursuit, and Jack would stay hidden in the bedroom.

"What do we do?" Tess asked.

Logan didn't have an answer.

Checking the rearview for traffic, his grip on the steering wheel tightened from what he saw.

In the back seat, the old toothless bag lady stared at him, laughing.

Lightning quick, her hands shot out and grabbed Logan by the throat.

Losing control of the wheel, he yelped as he tried to breathe, clawing at the hands tightening around his neck.

Tess tried to grab for the steering wheel to control the car, which veered across lanes, but his foot was slammed onto the accelerator.

There was no time, as the sedan hit the railings along the far right of the lane. A deafening screech of metal on metal shortly sounded as the car jolted, flipping over itself. Spinning through the air as it cleared the railing and fell down the embankment to the off-ramp below. The sound of twisting metal almost deafened them as the car thunderously collided to a stop.

———

Logan's eyes fluttered as he came to. Realizing what had happened.

Slowly and painfully, he lifted his head. He could see he was pinned against the wheel, his forehead bloody from the impact.

Glancing to his side, he could see that the passenger seat was empty. Tess was nowhere to be seen, and no old bag lady was in the back.

At a loss and in a daze, Logan exhaled as he released the seat belt and dragged himself out from the upturned car.

TRANSIT

In the lower level of the convent, Logan rushed down the stairs, having barged past the nun at the door. The blood on his forehead was drying but still staining his skin. He looked feral. No one could have stopped him from coming down here.

Banging on the same far left door, Logan furiously shouted, "Open up!"

The panel slot opened, revealing the shadowy silhouette of Sister Marguerite, still in her dimly candlelit room.

"I told you I have nothing more to say to you," she said.

Her voice was hoarse and tone was stern. She went to close the panel again, but Logan stopped it with his hand and pushed it back open.

"You wanna hide out from the rest of the world in this rat hole? I don't give a damn. But he has taken

Tess, and I'm not leaving until you help me. You know what these things are. What Channing is. And you can tell me what it is I can do."

"You have found one?" Marguerite asked calmly.

"Tell me how I can stop him. He must have some weakness. *Something!* He can't be unstoppable."

"He could not be."

"Then, what the hell do I have to do, huh?" He almost punched the door in frustration. "Tell me what I can do, and I'll do it!"

Marguerite's silhouette grew larger as she stepped closer to the door. "You would not stand a chance against a force like that. You are too weak to beat any being strong enough to come back with the First Power. I tried, and I had a dozen strong women of devout faith around me. I could not beat one."

"It doesn't matter what happens to me." Logan's voice fell to a whisper. "I have to help her."

As he spoke, Sister Marguerite leaned in nearer, her face coming into view. Her haunted expression looked at Logan's torment closely.

"You are telling the truth, aren't you? I thought you may be one of the liars who have come before, trying anything to get me to talk to them. But you... This is real."

Rushing down the stairs, a priest was flanked by two nuns, ready to drag Logan away. But Sister Marguerite noticed them coming and held up her hand through the panel, stopping them in their tracks. They held back.

He looked again at Logan. "Are you willing to die?"

"As long as I can stop this."

The door to her small room clicked as Sister Marguerite unlocked it and let Logan inside.

With a look of surprise, the priest turned and led the nuns back up the stairs.

The candle in her small bedroom flickered as Sister Marguerite unbuttoned the top of her habit. Opening the neckline, she lowered the fabric, showing a scar that lay beneath. The scar of a pentagram that had once been carved into her chest.

"I did not listen to the warnings," she explained. "I ran in headfirst and cocksure like you. And I lost everyone. Now I have a permanent reminder of what I did, what I caused. Who I'm responsible for the deaths for. Erik Kolfax may have been possessed by a dead man, but I was the one who chased him down. Who had faced evil when no one else could."

"What can I do?" Logan asked helplessly.

"There is only one way to stop him," she said as she turned to the small chest at the foot of her bed. From inside, she brought out a long object. She held it out to Logan. "It is how I finally freed Erik Kolfax of his curse. But he died along with it." She presented a pentagram lined at its bottom with razor-sharp blades pointing downward. The blades, when stabbed, would leave a perfect cut of the pattern, which aligned with the sister's wound. "I thought I had the strength to let it possess me. I thought I could sacrifice myself for the greater good, not sacrifice the poor soul it inhabited. And it worked. It transferred into me when I offered. It could not resist a nun. I felt its sickness. It's darkness. But I had to dig this blade deep into my chest, killing me and locking it inside forever."

She paused. "I tried. But I hesitated. I didn't push the blades in hard enough." She looked at Logan, her sadness evident. "It escaped. And because of me, seven souls lost their lives. And I was left alone. I pleaded to God to let me die, too... Please let me come with you."

————

The reservoir's concrete was exuding heat from its solid surface so much so that Logan could feel its intense rising temperature as he and Sister Marguerite crossed over to the spillway tunnel.

The tunnel itself was dark like before, even in the bright, warming summer sun. Inside, the heat was gone, and in its place, a deathly coldness. Logan had forgotten the stench of mold and rust from before as it hit his nostrils again. He grimaced as he peered back at Marguerite. She did not look bothered by it.

With his torch and pistol, he led the way through the darkness, up to the place where he and Tess had stopped before, and through the bent-up door and into the large room. He shined the torch into the low passageway ahead and carried on, to where the workman said a child once drowned.

The tunnel soon turned to steps as it went deeper down.

Walls were cracked, as if it was in a slow but losing battle with gravity, gradually being crushed under the weight of L.A.... The path was littered with chunks of debris that had crumbled off from these walls.

Around them, the constant *drip, drip, drip* of water accompanied their journey.

The smell of mold and rot was soon joined by another smell. A smell of stagnancy. A smell of abandonment. A desperate smell of age. It made him shiver as he walked on, feeling that the smells and sounds were becoming oppressive.

He did not even consider what he was doing. He was walking here, expecting everything to be fixed somehow. As if he only had to get here to solve his problems and to find and free Tess.

It was when they started down the next much shorter tunnel that Logan felt a sudden pull of panic. Ahead, far ahead, he could see a small pinprick of light. Ducking, he and Sister Marguerite walked slowly, farther and farther, deeper and deeper into the earthquake-damaged water system, to the light ahead of them.

Then, the tunnel opened into a much wider chamber. One lit with rows of large candles around the room. On each wall were multitudes of pentagrams and other occult symbols, each smeared in a browning red paste. As the stench in the chamber included the scents of copper and human waste, he could tell what the symbols were 'painted' in.

He nearly choked as he turned back to Sister Marguerite. "Stay behind me," he whispered, handing her the flashlight.

She nodded, her eyes wide and filled with a fear that she hadn't felt for decades.

Logan gripped his pistol as his gaze swept across the chamber. He scanned the entrances of several tunnels branching out from arched stone doorways that encircled the room. Down here, there was a distinct lack of earthquake damage, as if it missed this room by some miracle or curse.

The area felt labyrinthine. It was full of nooks and crannies, with hidden pockets of shadows. Its ceiling sloped in an intentionally irregular pattern, as if the necessities of the site dictated its construction, forgoing any expected aesthetic. This room was how it had to be. The floor was the same, lowering and rising, with steps leading to different leveled platforms.

Logan paced cautiously forward, on alert as he tried to be silent as he stepped.

Ahead, a pillar had been masking the center plat-form in this large chamber. Behind it, a large flat slab of concrete lay, where a thirty-foot pentagram was drawn in the same putrid muck as the graffiti on the walls.

Scattered around the area were various objects, wallets, photographs, bits of jewelry. Hundreds of items in all.

But in the center of it all, bound by rope attached to stakes, stripped naked with her legs and arms spread, an unconscious Tess lay.

Logan rushed over, lowering his guard for a second, but as he did, a weight smacked him over the head from behind, a flashlight colliding with his skull.

Collapsing to his knees, he peered back in a daze and saw the cruel grin of Sister Marguerite, changed from her usual stoicism into a fury.

"I brought him to you!" she screamed. Her voice reverberated through the chamber. "I thought he was a liar. Trying to find out our infernal secrets, but as soon as I realized he was telling the truth, I had to come. I *had* to join with you."

Her tone had shifted. A much more weaselly male voice.

There was no reply as Marguerite looked around, wild and expectantly.

"What—" Logan held his head, his vision swimming as he tried to regain his balance.

"Happs?"

Channing's baritone voice echoed throughout the chamber.

Marguerite, imbued with the spirit of Clive Happs, looked overjoyed. "I knew it!" she said in her possessed male voice. "I've been waiting so patiently for someone else to come. To show the way. To lead. All I have had to sustain me is the small bites from this holy bitch's soul. I have been trapped here for so long."

The bag lady soon appeared from the shadowed corner of the room with a chuckle. She walked over, carrying Channing's same undeniable swagger.

"I also brought you this gift," Marguerite said, offering up the bladed pentagram. "So, they cannot use it against you."

The bag lady approached and smiled at Marguerite, taking the bladed weapon from her. She then turned to Logan, who was crouched in front of Tess, trying to untie her.

"Buddy boy..." Channing's words rang out. "You know what I hate more than cops?"

Logan did not answer. He kept one dazed eye on them and one on untying Tess.

Soon, she was free but not yet conscious.

"Tess," he whispered as he gently tapped her face to rouse her.

"More than cops, I hate child killers." The bag lady's possessed voice was laced with a sudden disgust. As these words were spoken, Sister Marguerite's face fell in confusion. "Adults are fair game," the bag lady continued. "But not kids. Never kids."

With a sudden burst of anger, the bag lady grabbed the nun by her forehead, and in an instant, as if a power switch had been flicked, a thick black void shot out from the eyes and mouth of the nun as she screamed, Clive Happs screamed. The void quickly became darker and darker until, all of a sudden, it cut out, and the nun fell to the floor in a dead heap.

Happs was gone, and his hold on Sister Marguerite's body was released.

Turning back to Logan, the bag lady's anger shifted creepily to joy as her smile returned. "Amateur," she mumbled before speaking up. "So now, we do what we were meant to do." With that, she pulled out the familiar large, serrated knife from her belt.

Bang.

Logan fired a shot into the bag lady's chest.

But it had little effect. She just smiled and stepped closer.

Bang. Bang. Bang.

Four shots, each into the bag lady's head. Each one would've been a kill shot.

The bag lady laughed. "You don't get it, buddy boy," she said with great amusement. "I will destroy you."

"Why?" Logan asked through a haze, his teeth gritted tightly. "You wanted this, right?" He then spotted Tess's clothes in a pile to one side. Her jacket specifically.

"Why, you ask?" The bag lady laughed. "I think the question should be, why not? This is *fun*, that's why. This isn't about you. It's about your pain. Your torment. Your fear. You are just my random pick."

Logan paused. Random pick? Like his father's death?

She then launched herself at Logan, her expression terrifyingly angry as she pushed him backward to the ground. In an instant, she raised the knife and slammed it downward.

Logan jerked out of the way as the blade clinked off the concrete surface below. He then headbutted the possessed lady, kicked her off, and frantically reached for Tess's jacket.

The bag lady laughed in amusement as she turned after him. Her nose bleeding from the impact with his forehead.

Logan's hand shot up and pressed something hard against the bag lady's face. The pentagram amulet that had been in Tess's jacket pocket. As the metal hit her flesh, it burned like a branding.

The bag lady squealed in agony, reeling backward and grabbing her face. The amulet had seared into her cheek, burying itself deeper in her skin.

Logan looked in surprise, not realizing that could even happen, and by the bag lady's face, Channing didn't either.

Not missing a beat and not wanting to lose the upper hand, Logan staggered to his feet and ran over to Marguerite's dead body. From the floor, he grabbed the bladed pentagram in his free hand. Turning back to the bag lady, she glared at him with an intense, terrifying rage.

Logan barreled toward her.

"I will murder everyone you have ever known," the bag lady spat in anger.

Logan sneered back. "You think you're powerful? You're only a scared kid, aren't you? Still running from your grandpa? Or should I say *dad*?"

The bag lady screamed in fury as she ran at him, her blade held high.

Logan turned and ran in the opposite direction, away from the chamber, back up through the tunnels.

Logan considered the plan. He had the pentagram blade, but he needed to catch the bag lady off guard and not in an open space. So, he continued to lead her away from the chamber, up the tunnel, away from Tess.

Getting to the chamber above, Logan saw the metal wheels and remembered the workman's warning. As the bag lady appeared, Logan raised the pentagram blade in front of him. His arm lashed out as the bag lady advanced on him. The sharp metal sliced deeply through her neck with ease.

With an unearthly shriek, the bag lady grabbed the wound, from which a thick black smoke seeped out, like it had come out of Marguerite. But as it did, the bag lady's face shifted. Everything about her changed. Through her angered screams, her body convulsed.

"No," she screamed as her face continued to contort, her features twisting into that of Patrick Channing's.

Logan grabbed the metal wheel on the pole and

began to turn it. Opening the water valves. Then, onto a second one, he did the same.

Before either could do much more, a deep rumbling rang out around them. Neither had no time to react before the huge, powerful jet of water billowed out from the sides of the room, crisscrossing around them. Knocking them off their feet.

This rusted, stagnant water, which had been in the pipes for decades, flushed them down the tunnel.

Logan had tried to grip onto a pipe on the wall, to pull himself free, but he had nothing to grip. He and Channing tumbled back down to the chambers below.

As they were jettisoned back into the main chamber, the water rushed in.

The bag lady had shifted fully into Patrick Channing, and he looked incensed as he glanced around for the knife. But there was no time.

"Hey," Logan called out, "buddy boy."

Channing turned to him and—

Bang.

A bullet shot through one of Channing's eyes. Demolishing it on impact.

Bang.

Another bullet through his other eye.

Staggering and unable to see, he screamed in a defiant rage. Like a petulant child, his face turned even more sour.

Logan could not let up. He barged into Channing,

sending his blind body smashing into a large stone pillar behind him.

As Channing crumpled the floor, Logan was there, pentagram blade in hand, as he swiftly stabbed it down deep into Channing's heart.

His scream rang out, unnaturally loud, as the silver sliced through his organs. His expression of rage gave way to one of shock and terrified surprise.

Logan stood as Channing contorted beneath him, twisting with agony. The pentagram blades glowed white, as if being heated up from an unknown source. As they did, black smoke poured from Channing's eye sockets and mouth.

"No!" he screamed again.

Logan felt a hand grip his arm. Turning, with his gun raised, he relented as he saw Tess. Half dressed, looking weak and pained.

As fast as they could, they escaped the chamber, battling the torrent of water before it filled the room up anymore. Logan didn't know what to do. How could any of this be explained? What if the convent came asking where their nun was? And the bag lady? How did he even know what he did with the pentagram blade had even worked? He had nothing to show for it.

Glancing over his shoulder, he briefly considered retrieving Channing's body, to show people the proof, but the water was coming in faster and faster.

As they climbed through the torrent of water, a sudden scream pulled Logan out of his worry, as

Channing, eyeless with smoke still pouring out of him, leaped at them from behind.

In a quick second, Tess was wrenched back and dragged down an adjacent tunnel. One that was also being flooded with a larger jet of old water. This tunnel was steeply inclined as she tumbled down, like on a deathly amusement park ride. Channing gripped her wrist hard as he pulled her down after him, leaving Logan fearfully standing there.

The roaring, cascading water around them was deafening as Tess and Channing fell down this water-slide. As they moved, the only illumination was from shafts of sunlight that fell in through periodic grids in the ceiling, all of which shot by at an increasing speed.

His grip on Tess was so strong her flailing did nothing to stop her descent.

Ahead, another stream of sunlight could be seen. A stream accompanied by a deep, terrifying roar.

Tess screamed as she saw them, the large spinning blades of an industrial axial fan. Heavy blades spun and spun, having been triggered by the flood of water, whose sole purpose was to stop large objects from entering the drainage tunnels below by cutting them into smaller pieces.

Channing may not have been able to see the large blades closing in on them, but he knew what they were. He knew every part of this conduit.

At the last moment, as Tess screamed at what seemed like her imminent fate, Channing reached up and grabbed hold of a metal crossbar spanning the tunnel. As he did, smoke continued to ebb out of him. The more of it that did, the paler, gaunter Channing became and the weaker he got.

Tess tried to grab onto the pole, too, but she missed her mark. All she could do was grab onto Channing's body as tight as possible.

He growled as he tried to kick her off. But her weight pulled him down, forcing his grip to slip. He was getting too weak to hold on.

He then lifted his boot to apply a final kick at her. When Logan, using all the strength he had, came smashing down from the tunnel after them and into his torso, he managed to grab onto the metal crossbar.

Channing had no time to react as his grip was forced off from the metal bar. Logan reached down and grabbed Tess as Channing's body helplessly flew toward the hungry blades.

"Adios, buddy boy," Channing laughed as the blades cut through his entire body.

Slicing him up in a matter of milliseconds, it demolished his flesh and bone in an instant. The pentagram knife embedded in him, clanged as it hit the blades and then fell into the deep water below.

Logan, holding tightly onto Tess, peered up at the grid of light shining down from above.

An exit. An escape.

But just as he prepared to climb, to lead them to

safety, just as the taste of freedom was within reach... a deep, thunderous rumble rolled through the tunnel.

The sound wasn't just noise; it was a warning.

Then came the roar.

Not like the rushing currents that had already dragged them down her, tumbling them through the tunnels. This was something else. An unrelenting force of nature. The water system had fully ruptured, and everything it had held back, every ton of pent-up destruction, was surging toward them.

It slammed into the walls with the sound of a freight train, a wall of fury swallowing everything in its path. The force was far beyond anything they could fight. There would be no gaps to breathe through this time. No lucky pockets of air. This would fill the tunnels completely.

Logan turned to Tess, his soaked fingers tightening around her wrist.

She met his gaze, her breath shallow, her body trembling with exhaustion.

No words were needed.

One last embrace. One last connection.

Then, the water consumed them.

Darkness.

Tess didn't open her eyes right away. Awareness crept in slowly, carried by the gentle brush of wind against her face. A fleeting moment of peace, before a pain crept through her body.

When she finally forced her eyes open, the blinding sunlight above made her wince. She was soaked, bruised, and broken, as she tried to figure out where she was, and what had happened. Somewhere in the distance, she could hear the mechanical roar of a still-spinning fan echoed. Turning her head to the left she saw a wall broken apart where the water had burst through, carrying them outside. The furious wave had become an ineffectual trickling, that seeped into the grass around her.

She then turned to look at the other side of her. A sharp gasp escaped her lungs, as there, lying next to her, was Logan.

He was deathly pale.

Motionless.

Not breathing.

———

'Breaking news out of Los Angeles tonight, shocking revelations in the case of the Pentagram Killer. In a joint statement released this hour, the Mayor together with the Police Commissioner confirmed that Lieutenant Jonah Grimes, who had been leading the investigation into the Pentagram Killer case, is now revealed to have been orchestrating the copycat crimes following the execution

of the original killer, Patrick Channing. This develop-
ment has sent shockwaves through both law enforcement
and the public, raising serious questions about how and
why Grimes was operating undetected for so long.'

The television in the hospital room switched off.

Propped up in a hospital bed, Logan set down the
remote, grimacing as a sharp pain tore through his
body. Bruises covered him, a plaster clung to his fore-
arm, and a bandage was wrapped tightly across his
chest.

He looked dazed, drugged. His eyes started to
close.

"You've really been through this," a voice suddenly
said.

Logan's eyes snapped back open.

It was Perkins, seated in the chair beside the bed.
"Four broken ribs, cracked wrist, concussion. They said
you had so many opioids in your system, it's probably
the only reason you survived."

"I'll be fine," Logan replied as he glanced around,
bleary-eyed, as though waking from a nightmare.

Perkins looked at him dubiously. "Let's hope so,"
he replied. "Anyway, I got you what you asked for." He
pulled a VHS tape from his jacket. "You can have this
on one condition, you drop that nonsense about
Channing coming back from the dead." He leaned in.
"Just take the win, Logan. You're getting a promotion,
and the media's eating up the Grimes copycat story.

Keep talking about Channing, and you'll end up in the psych ward across the street."

Logan didn't answer.

Perkins sighed, walked over to the television and slid the VHS into the tape slot beneath the screen. The television soon flickered to life, showing grainy black-and-white footage of a hospital entrance. For several seconds, nothing happened... then a car rolled into view.

Logan's eyes narrowed. On-screen, a limping Tess emerged from the driver's seat. Even with the poor-quality video, her pain was obvious. She circled the car, her right arm hanging uselessly at her side as she struggled to open the passenger door. She finally dragged the unconscious Logan's body out of the car and onto the ground, before getting back behind the wheel and speeding away.

"Tess brought me here?" Logan's asked as his thoughts reeled. "Have you questioned her?"

Perkins shook his head grimly. "We checked her apartment, asked around with her friends... nothing. It's like she vanished. You don't think she was involved, do you?"

"Involved?" Logan said. "No, she couldn't be."

"Okay, I'll take your word for it. But I hope she's a million miles away. The last thing we need is that lunatic popping up again saying she predicted all this."

Logan coughed, spasming as if struggling to breathe.

Perkins handed him a glass of water from the bedside table, as he studied him with concern. "Look, you need to rest. I'll come back to see you as soon as I can, alright?"

Taking a sip of the water, Logan set the glass back on the table and then lay back as his eyes began to close.

The door soon clicked shut, as Perkins left.

After a moment, Logan swung his legs over the edge of the bed and stood up, making his way slowly to the bathroom.

Shutting the door behind him, he turned to look in the mirror.

Suddenly, he seemed different.

A strange smile crept across his face. His posture straightened as though his injuries had vanished. He stared at his reflection—but it wasn't *exactly* his reflection. The figure in the mirror wasn't smiling. Instead, it was silently screaming, eyes wide with horror.

It was Detective Russell Logan.

The *real* Logan. Trapped behind the glass, terrified at the sight of the thing now controlling his body. Patrick Channing.

"I hate to see this end," the presence in Logan's body murmured. "But it's time, isn't it? You know that." His brow furrowed as if struck by an odd thought. "I'm gonna miss you," he said, then paused, tilting his head. "Won't I?"

He exhaled, dismissing the notion, and a sharper,

more malevolent smile spread over his features. "I mean I'll have plenty to do. I can run around in this cop suit all day—wear the flesh down until it's ragged and dead. Or until they catch me, and I move on again." He leaned closer to the screaming Logan in the mirror. "I'll try you on for a while, at least until your flesh heals and I can have some fun. What did that psychic say? You can't keep killing forever?" He scoffed. "I *think* I can. Hell, I gotta try, right?" His expression turned serious. "Maybe I'll find her first. I always thought she had kind of a thing for me."

The Logan trapped in the mirror silently screamed again, begging anyone or anything for help, but he was now in a world far beyond anyone's reach.

Channing, inhabiting Logan's flesh, paused for a moment, then slowly lifted his hand. He carefully pressed his fingers against the glass. Inside the reflection, Logan is pushed backward, his body suddenly dragged into the mirror's void, as a surrounding blackness came in from all sides to consume him. Swallowing him up. Extinguishing him from all contact with reality.

Channing, now the *only* Logan, watched impassively as the mirror's reflection vanished, leaving only an absolute blackness.

"See ya 'round, buddy boy," he said.

Also Available

Official Novelizations
by Christian Francis

Session 9: The Official Novelization

978-1-916582-59-0 (eBook)

978-1-916582-60-6 (Paperback)

978-1-916582-61-3 (Hardcover)

————

Maniac Cop 1, 2 & 3 (*May* 2025)

Night of the Comet (2025)

The Gate (2025)

Dee Snider's Strangeland (2025)

3615 Code Père Noël aka **Deadly Games** (2025)

In The Mouth of Madness (2025)

Tremors (2025)

plus many more to be announced.

From other publishers

The Descent (*Titan Publishing Group*) - Oct 2025

Wishmaster (*Encyclopocalypse*) - Out now

Vamp (*Encyclopocalypse*) - Out now

Creature, aka **Titan Find** (*Encyclopocalypse*) - Out now

Original Novels and Novellas
by Christian Francis

The Dead Woods

YA Horror

978-1-916582-00-2 (eBook)

978-1-916582-02-6 (Paperback)

978-1-916582-04-0 (Hardcover)

★★★★★

"One of the best YA books I have ever read."

David W Adams (Amazon)

The Devil and The Deep

Cosmic Horror

978-1-916582-52-1 (eBook)

978-1-916582-55-2 (Paperback)

978-1-916582-54-5 (Hardcover)

The Sacrifice of Anton Stacey

Horror Novella

978-1-916582-06-4 (eBook)

979-8-386183-59-2 (Paperback)

Everyday Monsters - The Animus Chronicles 1

Dark Fantasy / Horror

978-1-916582-03-3 (eBook)

978-1-916582-09-5 (Paperback)

978-1-916582-10-1 (Hardcover)

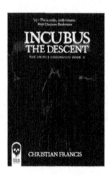

Incubus: The Descent - The Animus Chronicles 2

Dark Fantasy / Horror

978-1-916582-08-8 (eBook)

978-1-916582-11-8 (Paperback)

978-1-916582-12-5 (Hardcover)

Anti Rule: Navigating The Lies About Fiction Writing

Non-Fiction

978-1-916582-01-9 (eBook)

978-1-916582-05-7 (Paperback)

Two worlds at war will bring them together... or tear them apart...

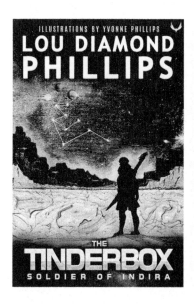

From the imagination of actor Lou Diamond Phillips (*La Bamba, Stargate Universe, Prodigal Son*) comes an epic and unforgettable Science Fantasy tale.

Imagine the intrigue of *Game of Thrones* mixed with the star-crossed romance of *Romeo and Juliet*... but in space!

Available as ebooks, paperbacks, harcovers and audiobooks!

Grab your copies today!

Printed in Great Britain
by Amazon

61918204R00161